Published by
Fugitive Poets Press
Greensboro, NC

Copyright © 2014 John Leslie Butchart

First Edition

ISBN: 9781938045028

Back panel photo of Ariel Burke was taken by Mark Robertson.

Lake of Fire

a feature screenplay by

John Leslie Butchart

FUGITIVE POETS PRESS
Greensboro, North Carolina

for my Wildacres Friends

Acknowledgments: I want to thank my son, Lucas, for the extremely helpful critique he gave the third draft of this screenplay. Thanks also to my friends Matt Nunn and Hugh Spinks for providing a constant flow of advice and encouragement.

A Word of Warning:

Be careful what you wish for (as a screenwriter) because one day you just might have to go out and make the movie you wrote!

I am grateful to Fugitive Poets Press for this opportunity to bring the script for *Lake of Fire* to readers, especially those readers who are interested in how movies evolve.

This screenplay went through seven major drafts and many minor drafts thereafter, eleven in all, but this draft is the one that has "the whole enchilada," the story I wanted to tell, or thought I wanted to tell until we had to figure out how to make it. The making of a film can be painful, especially for the writer-director who gets to see his own work brutalized by the process. And who also gets to see it brought to life in new ways by wonderfully talented people like cinematographer Philip Dann, who made our movie look incredible, and wonderful actors like Ariel Burke, Billy Ingram, Chris Best, Doug Brown, Logan Anderson, Andrea Powell, Michael Vadini, Jason Blackman, Judi Hill, Slade Blackburn, Jeffrey Wall, Brian Mullins, Hannah Kirby ... and all the other great actors who worked their magic on these words.

I suggest you see the movie version of this screenplay after reading it. I think you'll be impressed by the way the story comes to life on the screen.

Either one is serious about salvation or one is not. And it is well to realize that the maximum amount of seriousness admits the maximum amount of comedy.

"Novelist and Believer" (1963)
-- Flannery O'Connor

EXT. HOLLIS HOUSE -- SHERIFF CLANCY & HOWARD -- DAY
A run-down, shack-like structure. The Sheriff's cruiser pulls up and
Sheriff Carl Clancy gets out and walks toward the house. Howard, a
crusty farmer, opens the front door, a cold beer in his hand.

> **SHERIFF**
> Howard? What are you doing?

> **HOWARD**
> I was just helping myself to a cold one. That
> boy's not gonna need 'em.

> **SHERIFF**
> What boy is that?

> **HOWARD**
> The boy what lived here.

> **SHERIFF**
> Get out of there. If this is a crime scene you
> already messed it up.

> **HOWARD**
> I didn't mess up anything, Carl.

> **SHERIFF**
> Go on, get out ...

INT. HOLLIS HOUSE -- SHERIFF
The Sheriff goes inside, looks around. The TV is on.

> **SHERIFF**
> Did you turn this TV on?

Howard is standing outside, looks through the door.

> **HOWARD**
> No, didn't touch a thing.

The Sheriff goes to the bedroom. The mattress and pillows are
covered in blood. RAY SPECKLE is on the TV, preaching, the volume
on low. The Sheriff walks closer to the bed, a wallet lies at his feet, spread
open -- he picks it up, checks the contents, I.D. card, etc. The Sheriff

1

walks back into the living room, then into the kitchen, looks around. Gets himself a beer. Thinks, drinks. Goes outside.

EXT. HOUSE -- SHERIFF AND HOWARD
Howard is still outside when the Sheriff comes out.

> **SHERIFF**
> Boy's name was Larry who lived here?

> **HOWARD**
> That's right.

> **SHERIFF**
> What do you know about him?

> **HOWARD**
> Not much. Just seen him around some.

> **SHERIFF**
> Lived alone?

> **HOWARD**
> Far as I know.

The Sheriff walks around to the back of the house where a rusted old fifty-gallon trash barrel is smoking. He pauses and studies the ground. Then he walks up to the barrel tentatively, looks down into it, makes a face because of the bad smell, raises his arm to cover his nose. A twig snaps. The Sheriff's head turns toward the woods. We see nothing. The Sheriff turns and looks at Howard, picks up a stick, and turns back to the barrel. He puts a handkerchief to his nose and looks down into the barrel. He finds something in there and fishes it out. It's a skull. He puts it on the ground.

A half hour later, the Sheriff has found other bones. They are arranged on the ground, charred black, ash-covered. Howard walks up with two more beers, one for himself, one he hands to the Sheriff.

> **HOWARD**
> Dear Mother of God.

> **SHERIFF**
> Yeah.

They hear a rustling sound and the Sheriff looks up.

SHERIFF'S P.O.V. -- A PIT BULL
The dog, a handsome, broad-shouldered brown male, stands there about thirty feet away, a bloody knife in its mouth.

SCENE WITH SHERIFF AND HOWARD

                    SHERIFF
          Drop it, boy. Come on now, be a good dog and
          drop it.

The dog drops it and the Sheriff is pleased. The dog runs off. The Sheriff picks up the knife using his handkerchief, opens a plastic bag and slips it inside.

INT. HOLLIS HOUSE -- SHERIFF
He walks back inside the trailer, to the kitchen, and looks at the knife block. One of the knives is missing. He looks at the knife in the baggie. It's the knife that belongs in the knife block, so he knows it was probably the murder weapon.

(During this sequence, Ray is seen on TV preaching hellfire for sinners and salvation for believers in his own inimitable style of televangelism.)

EXT. DOWNTOWN CHARLOTTE -- RAY SPECKLE AND CROWD -- DAY -- (48 DAYS LATER)
In the sidewalk, Ray waves his big black Bible in the air. He wears shiny red cowboy boots, a bolo tie and white cowboy hat. A few people have actually stopped to listen.

GRAPHIC: 48 DAYS LATER

CUT TO THE CARDBOARD CHICKEN BUCKET AT HIS FEET
He's earned a few coins and a one dollar bill.

EXT. DINER -- RAY -- LATER
Forlorn, he drinks a cup of coffee while counting his change.

INT. ITALIAN KITCHEN IN CHARLOTTE- LUCY--THAT NIGHT
Lucy, a pretty red-headed country girl, age 23, works as a bus girl and dishwasher, hustling plates from dining room to kitchen and loading the dishwasher.

INT. BUS -- LUCY -- LATER
Worn out, she rides home.

INT. HOTEL ROOM -- RAY -- THAT NIGHT
A cheap, dingy old motel room. There are two single beds. Wearing a wife-beater, Ray sits at a table near a window. Neon lights blink outside the windows. He drinks whiskey, reads his Bible and takes notes.

CUT TO SHERIFF'S FEET ON THE HOTEL STAIRWAY
As he climbs the stairs.

ANOTHER ANGLE ON THE SHERIFF IN THE HALLWAY
He stops at the door to Ray's room.

JIB UP FROM HIS HANDS WITH KEYS TO HIS FACE
As the Sheriff opens the door, and this is the first time we really know it's him, as he opens the door ...

SHERIFF'S P.O.V. -- RAY
Ray sits at the table as before, looks up.

BACK TO ANGLES ON SHERIFF AND RAY

> **RAY**
>Hello Carl.

> **SHERIFF**
>Ray. I think you know why I'm here.

> **RAY**
>You come a long way.

> **SHERIFF**
>Yes I did.

Ray slides the bottle of whiskey toward the Sheriff.

> **RAY**
>I just cracked the stamp on this boy.

> **SHERIFF**
>Bring it with you. It's going to be a long ride.

4

The Sheriff sees a suitcase at the end of one of the beds, reaches into it and pulls out a pair of women's underwear.

SHERIFF
Where is she, Ray?

EXT. CHARLOTTE STREET -- MARKET -- LUCY
She comes out of the all-night market carrying a small sack of groceries. Two black kids follow her. She stops and faces them. They stop.

LUCY
You been keeping' your eyes open?

BOYS
Don't we always.

She reaches into the sack and hands the boys a pack of cigarettes. One of the boys opens it. They each take a cigarette then offer one to Lucy.

BOY ONE
Who you looking' for anyhow? You in trouble with the police?

LUCY
It ain't worth talkin' bout, really it ain't.

BOY TWO
It ain't, huh. Why, you kill somebody?

LUCY
That's none of your business.

BOY ONE
You married to that old street preacher?

LUCY
No.

BOY TWO
What, is he your pimp?

LUCY
He's my daddy if you wanna know.

BOY TWO
(mocking her) Yer *daddy.* Ain't that sweet.

She makes a face at them, they smile.

BOYS
Peace out, Lucy.

LUCY
Peace out.

CUT TO HOTEL HALLWAY AND LUCY -- LATER
She comes toward the room carrying the groceries.

ANGLE ON HALLWAY AND SHERIFF
The Sheriff comes out of the hotel room, and Lucy freezes.

SHERIFF
Hi Lucy.

The Sheriff sets Ray's suitcase in the hallway, then he pulls Ray out of the room. He's in handcuffs, and he has a cowboy shirt on, unbuttoned.

LUCY
You wanna put me in handcuffs, too?

SHERIFF
No, just get your things.

The light is harsh in the hallway. A sad-looking couple walks by. Ray leans against the hallway wall as Lucy goes into the room. Lucy puts stuff into her suitcase.

SHERIFF
I ain't never. Had to run off to the Queen City.

Ray looks at Lucy, Lucy at him.

SHERIFF
I swear, you two take the cake.

EXT. NORTH CAROLINA COUNTRYSIDE -- GREYHOUND
Our view is of the front of the bus.

GRAPHIC: A YEAR LATER

INT. -- GREYHOUND BUS -- LUCY SPECKLE -- AFTERNOON
The wind catches Lucy's long red hair and obscures her face, the land-
scape flashes by in the window.

CLOSE-UP OF LUCY'S BROWN EYES

LUCY'S P.O.V. -- COUNTRYSIDE -- RURAL NORTH CAROLINA
Horses in pasture, farmers in the field, watering systems wetting down
cropland, kids playing in dusty front yards.

EXT. DOWNTOWN RAMSEUR, NC -- LUCY
Hardly a downtown at all. An old grocery store, hardware store, tractor
store, tiny post office and Mexican church. The year is 2007. Lucy steps
off the bus. Her hair blows into her mouth, she spits it out.

> **TODD BENSON (V.O.)**
> Sometimes trouble comes disguised in a pretty
> package. So it was with Lucy, who did her time
> at county correctional, and came home to a
> place that wasn't ready to get her back, a one
> light town stuck somewhere between stop and
> go. Lucy Speckle, oh she was a piece of work.

Just out of prison, she stands at curb with her suitcase beside her.

TITLE: **Lake of Fire**

CREDITS:

INT. JANEY'S CAR -- JANEY -- SAME TIME
Janey, age 45, an attractive, middle-age woman with a streak of propriety,
sings a hymn as she drives to town in a well-used, muddy-wheeled Bronco.

EXT. DOWNTOWN RAMSEUR, NC -- LUCY AND JANEY
Janey pulls to the curb and gets out.

> **JANEY**
> Hey sugar. Sorry it took me so long. Let's put
> that in the back seat.

> **LUCY**
> I got it.

Janey pauses, looks at Lucy.

> **JANEY**
> I forgot the most important thing.

She gives Lucy a polite hug and kiss on the cheek.

> **JANEY**
> How you doin'?

> **LUCY**
> I'm alright.

> **JANEY**
> My god, I think prison made you prettier.

> **LUCY**
> **(getting in the car)**
> Oh, I doubt that.

They drive away.

> **JANEY (O.C.)**
> My, your hair's grown a foot I bet.

EXT. TODD AND JANEY'S HOUSE -- LATER
The Bronco is parked in the driveway.

INT. TODD AND JANEY'S HOUSE -- JANEY AND LUCY
Lucy plops her big suitcase on the bed. Janey stands in the doorway while Lucy unpacks. Lucy lays a white Bible on the bedspread.

> **LUCY**
> **(stretching)**
> Oh god, I'm home.

> **JANEY**
> **(referring to the Bible)**
> That's nice to see.

> **LUCY**
> What? The Bible?

JANEY
It's got your name in gold.

Lucy picks it up, opens it.

LUCY
All the words that Jesus said are in red inside.

JANEY
You want some air in here?

Janey crosses the room and opens a window. Lucy looks at her Bible.

LUCY
I have a place to write down my matrimony day and spaces for my childrens' names when I have some. I've been wondering if I'll ever have any days or names to write in here.

JANEY
Try to be patient dear.

LUCY
Patient? I'm *twenty-three.* (beat) How come you and Uncle Todd never had any kids?

JANEY
We didn't need any, I guess. Or so God thought. (beat) That Bible will sure make your father proud.

LUCY
I ain't carryin' it for his sake.

JANEY
Well. I'll put supper on the table about five.

LUCY
You want I'll give you a hand.

JANEY
No, sugar, you relax, take a long bath or something.

LUCY

A *bath*, that sounds good.

INT. KITCHEN -- JANEY -- LATER

She is preparing dinner, working at the sink -- she looks out the window.

JANEY'S P.O.V. OF LUCY AND TODD OUTSIDE

Lucy sits on a rusted swing set, smoking a cigarette. Janey's husband (Lucy's uncle) Todd Benson, comes home from work. He is a house builder, a ruggedly handsome man. Lucy runs up to him and gives him a big hug as he lifts her off the ground and swings her in a circle.

ANGLE ON JANEY LOOKING WORRIED

JANEY
(to God, in exasperation)

Lord, if you want to take me now it would be alright.

INT. KITCHEN -- JANEY, TODD & LUCY -- LATER

They are seated, ready to eat. Todd extends a hand to each of them.

TODD

You want to give thanks?

LUCY

Okay. God, thank you for Uncle Todd and Aunt Janey and for gettin' me out early. Thank you in addition for this home-cooked food that smells like heaven. Amen.

TODD

Don't guess the food's too good where you've been.

LUCY

It's pretty much hog slop, but you learn to choke it down.

JANEY

You look a tad skinny to me.

LUCY

I must've lost ten pounds.

TODD

Six months didn't treat you too poorly.

JANEY

I could stand to lose ten pounds.

LUCY

But you don't want to go to women's correctional to do it, Janey.

TODD

You give any thought to what kind of job you might look for?

LUCY

Anything really.

TODD

Fred Graham needs a check out girl. He's put a sign in the window.

JANEY

At the hardware store? That's not a job for a young girl. Too many young bucks.

TODD

She's right about that.

LUCY

So? (laughs) I like young bucks.

JANEY

Lucy. Watch out.

LUCY

I do like 'em. (laughs) I mean, I been in Yancey County Correctional for six months. There's nothing in there but lesbos.

JANEY

My god.

LUCY

It's sad.

A car horn honks outside.

TODD

Who's that?

Lucy goes to the kitchen door, looks out.

LUCY

Pro'bly Carla.

JANEY

What's she want?

LUCY

We're goin' out.
(yelling to Carla)
Come inside, I ain't ready.

TODD

Out where?

LUCY

Out wherever, I guess.

CARLA enters through the kitchen door.

CARLA

Hey girl.

Carla and Lucy hug.

CARLA

Hey ya'll, how's everybody?

LUCY

I still gotta get dressed. Come on.

The girls walk down the hallway.

TODD

She just wants to spread her wings.

JANEY

She's not a bird. And surely not an angel.

TODD

Let her have some fun.

JANEY

Like I could stop her?

EXT. THE INFERNO -- LATER THAT NIGHT
A cinderblock juke joint with a neon sign.

INT. THE INFERNO -- LUCY & CARLA & CROWD
This place has a cement floor, wooden tables and ladder back chairs,
a simple, country place illuminated by beer signage. The girls order a
pitcher. Carla's useless boyfriend, CODY, comes over to their table.

LUCY AND CARLA DANCING -- SOME TIME LATER
The girls dance with each other to a tune by The Avett Brothers.

Later, the girls are sitting at a table, drinking beer, when CODY, Carla's
boyfriend, comes over with a guy name STUMP, and introduces him to
Lucy.

LUCY

Your name is *Stump?*

CODY

His old man owns the lumber mill.

CARLA

Stump's his nickname.

EXT. THE INFERNO -- LUCY AND CARLA -- LATER
They light up a joint out behind the place.

CARLA

You know I've heard people talking about you.

LUCY

What did they say about me?

CARLA

They say Lucy Speckle is a badass girl.

LUCY

Well, I am.

CARLA

Do you feel like, I don't know, like a *criminal?*

LUCY

I am a criminal. But I done my time.

CARLA

So you got a new life now.

LUCY
(sucking on the joint)

A new life. Yep.

CARLA

That's great, Lucy ... wow, your whole life is out
there ahead of you like when we graduated from
high school and everything was ... you know ...
up in the air. Hot damn, how great is that!

CODY and Stump come outside to join them.

STUMP

You girls want to really get wasted, I've got some
crystal.

LUCY
(ignoring Stump)

Come on Carla, let's go dance some more.

INT. THE INFERNO -- LUCY & CARLA AND CROWD -- LATER
Lucy dances like a crazy woman in a pentacostal church.

NEW ANGLE -- SHERIFF CLANCY
The Sheriff walks up to Lucy, who stops dancing and tries to catch her
breath. Sweat pours off her.

SHERIFF

I heard you got home.

LUCY

Yessir, I did.

SHERIFF

Why don't we sit down.

They sit down. The Sheriff sits close so she'll hear him.

> **SHERIFF**
> I see prison didn't put a damper on your party
> spirit.

> **LUCY**
> Oh, I couldn't let 'em do that to me.

> **SHERIFF**
> Anyhow, after what you been through, Lucy, you
> deserve some fun.

> **LUCY**
> I plan to get just as shit-faced as possible.

> **SHERIFF**
> That's it. Well ...

He stands, studies her for another moment, then he leans real low and speaks into her ear.

> **SHERIFF**
> There's some folks here bouts who are troubled
> by your short visit in county, thinking, I s'pose,
> you shoulda got more time. Just ... watch out for
> people with negative views.

> **LUCY**
> Okay. I will do that, Sheriff.

As the SHERIFF EXITS, Lucy sips her beer, licks foam off her lips.

INT. GUEST BEDROOM -- LUCY -- NEXT MORNING
Badly hungover, she is awakened by the sound of Janey mowing the lawn. Janey pushes the lawn mower past the window.

INT. KITCHEN -- LUCY AND TODD -- LATER
The mower can still be heard outside when Lucy walks into the kitchen. Todd is sitting at the table reading the paper. As Lucy gets coffee, Todd notices her long legs. All she's wearing is a baggy t-shirt that barely covers her underpants.

> **TODD**
> Wearing your undies around the house, Lucy,
> not a good idea.

15

LUCY
(sipping coffee)
Really? Why?

TODD
Let me put it to you this way, darlin', if Janey
saw you struttin' around in your underwear,
you'd be on her dark side automatic-like.

LUCY
Well, she's mowin' now, so I'm gonna sit here
and eat this tomater slice.

Lucy eats a slice of tomato.

INT. HARDWARE STORE -- LUCY & OTHERS -- LATER
When Lucy walks to the back of the hardware store, Fred Graham, the
proprietor, is socializing with a group of men. Her lithe figure and red
hair catch their eyes all at once and track her in unison.

LUCY
I'm lookin' for Mr. Graham.

FRED GRAHAM
I'm Fred Graham.

LUCY
I'm Todd Benson's niece, Lucy. He buys a lot of
wood and nails and stuff here. He builds houses.
(to the gathered men)
Hey everybody.
(to Fred Graham))
I hear you're lookin' for somebody to help out
here at the hardware. Would you consider givin'
me the job?

FRED GRAHAM
I would consider it, sure.

LUCY
You'd consider it but you wouldn't do it, 'cause I
been to prison.

FRED GRAHAM
I didn't say that, Lucy.

LUCY

Bet you were thinkin' it.

FRED GRAHAM

Lucy, it's not every day I run into a psychic like you who can read my mind.

LUCY

It's just common sense. Nobody wants to hire an ex-con.

FRED GRAHAM

What that boy did to you was ... well, it was *awful,* nobody blames you.

LUCY

Well, I'm glad they don't. It was one really bad day.

FRED GRAHAM

You shouldn't have to carry that curse with you forever.

LUCY

Nossir. I don't plan to.

He thinks for a moment.

FRED GRAHAM

Let me introduce you to Betty.

The men in the back of the hardware store watch as Fred introduces Lucy to an older woman named Betty. Apparently, Betty has been put in charge of Lucy's job orientation. Two men step up beisde Fred Graham.

MAN ONE

(to Fred) You better think twice, son.

FRED GRAHAM

Nobody asked you.

MAN TWO

Can you trust her?

FRED GRAHAM
I figure so, she didn't steal anything …

MAN TWO
No, she murdered that boy.

FRED GRAHAM
He raped her didn't he.

They admire Lucy's figure as she moves and bends in tight-fitting jeans.

MAN ONE
She's a spunky girl. Could make a fine employee.

MAN TWO
It would be mighty noble of you to give the girl
a chance.

Betty comes marching to the back of the store. She wears a concerned
look on her face.

FRED GRAHAM
What do you think of her?

BETTY
I don't like her. I don't trust her. She's a mur-
derer, for goshsake. Her type is trouble.

FRED GRAHAM
Betty, tell me, what is her type?

BETTY
You know, the white trash type.

A minute later, Fred approaches Lucy, who is busy arranging merchan-
dise. He glances over his shoulder at the men in the back and at Betty.

FRED GRAHAM
I can give you thirty hours a week to start.

LUCY
You mean I'm hired? Thank you.

She gives him a big, prolonged hug.

Later, Lucy stands near a window that looks into the lumber yard. She sees SAMSON, the black man who works in the lumber yard, greeting his PASTOR who has driven up in a shiny Lincoln Continental. Lucy turns to Betty.

> **LUCY**
> Who's that?

> **BETTY**
> That's Samson.

> **LUCY**
> Who's that other man in the big car?

> **BETTY**
> That's Samson's pastor. He's paying a visit because Samson's wife has cancer.

> **LUCY**
> Cancer? Oh my God.

Lucy watches as the two men pray together in the lumber shed.

INT. HARDWARE STORE -- LUCY, BETTY & SAMSON -- LATER
Samson enters and files the paperwork for a few lumber orders.

> **LUCY**
> Hello.

> **BETTY**
> That's Lucy.

> **LUCY**
> Lucy Speckle.

> **SAMSON**
> Speckle? Like something shiny. Hello Lucy. So, you're working with us now?

> **LUCY**
> Um-hm. I'm sorry about your wife. It's not easy losing somebody.

> **SAMSON**
> Well, I don't plan to *lose* her.

LUCY

But if you were to, it would be hard. What's her name? I'll put her in my prayers.

SAMSON

Her name is Becky.

Samson moves toward the door.

LUCY

I lost my momma.

SAMSON

I'm sorry to hear that.

LUCY

That's okay, I was real little. I hardly even remember her.

EXT. TODD AND JANEY'S HOUSE -- PORCH -- DUSK
A quiet, peaceful evening. Janey is rocking in a Kennedy rocker and Lucy is swinging in a bench swing at the end of the porch. A car stops in front of the house, a big, long 80's era Oldsmobile with peeling paint and large patches of rust.

JANEY

(calling) Todd, hey Todd!

Todd comes to the screen door.

JANEY

Who is that?

TODD

Hell if I know.

JANEY

I don't like them sittin' out there like that.

Todd disappears.

JANEY

Todd!

Todd returns with a wheelgun and walks to the middle of the front yard.

TODD
Get out of here! Go on!

The car doesn't budge. Todd raises the gun.

TODD
Want some more holes in that piece of shit?

When the car doesn't move, Todd shoots into the ground near it.

INT. CAR -- CLOSE-UP OF A HAND
A few grains of dirt are sprayed through the window when the bullet hits the ground. A hand brushes the dirt off the seat. Then the same hand snaps its middle finger and thumb.

CUT TO THE BACK WINDOW
As a PIT BULL lunges at the glass growling fiercely.

TODD'S REACTION
As he backs up.

CUT TO JANEY AND LUCY'S REACTION
As they flinch.

THEN BACK TO TODD
As the car finally begins to creep away.

CUT TO THE PORCH -- TODD, JANEY AND LUCY
As Todd returns.

JANEY
That was real smooth.

TODD
What?

JANEY
It's just ... that was real dumb. They're going
to come back sometime when your truck isn't
parked in the driveway and probably rape me n'
Lucy to death.

TODD

Rape you to death, huh.
(extending the gun)
You know how to use this?

JANEY

You know I do.

TODD

Good.

LUCY

What about me?

TODD

We'll do some target practice Saturday, how's
that. We'll kill us some Spaghetti-O cans.

LUCY

Really? Are you pulling my leg?

Todd goes inside.
(half-yelling)
Thank you Uncle Todd!

INT. COUNTY FARM -- RAY SPECKLE & OTHER INMATES --
SUNDAY MORNING
An old black man, JESSIE, prepares the communion elements in the
kitchen of the rustic county work farm, and adjacent to the kitchen, in
the dining hall, Ray Speckle is preaching the Sunday sermon. Jessie can
hear him -- he nods and smiles in agreement.

Jessie brings the elements into into the dining area.

RAY

And here's where the rubber meets the road my
fellow laborers. There is a river ... I say, there is
a river, and it runs with blood, that's right, a rich
red river of blood, and it's for all of us rough
beasts that the river flows forth, and its the river
we can lay our pain in. Will you lay down today
in that river of pain? We come here for Jesus
today friends, that's why we come. So his blood
can make us clean.

One of the inmates is glaring at Ray. When Ray finishes preaching, he
nods to a black inmate named Cliff, who stands and sings a hymn aca-
pella. Ray walks over to the man who has been glaring at him.

RAY
What is it, brother. What's got you so down?

INMATE
I know who you are. My momma gave you
money. She saw you on TV.

RAY
Well, God bless her then, and God bless you,
brother. Giving is a good thing, a good thing.
Indeed it is.

EXT. HOLLIS HOUSE -- LESTER & CHANCE -- DAY
Lester, a strange man of quiet ways, and his pit bull, Chance, walk across
the backyard of the ramshackle house deep in the country, to get some
firewood. (The P.O.V. of a window on the second story of the house.)

INT. HOLLIS HOUSE -- LESTER AND CHANCE
They come inside where the wood cookstove is crackling and a steak
is frying in a battered steel frying pan. Lester shoves more wood in the
stove. When the steak is done, he puts it on a plate. Chance sits patiently
watching, slobbering. Lester cuts the steak into tiny pieces and occasion-
ally tosses a piece to the pit bull.

Later, Lester carries a tray with the steak and a bottle of ketchup and
three slices of white bread upstairs, Chance trots up the stairs behind
him.

INT. ROOM -- LESTER, CHANCE & LESTER'S FATHER
His father is very old with a long white beard. His false teeth sit in a glass
beside his chair. A banjo leans against the wall. Lester puts the tray on
the old man's lap. His father begins to eat, making grunting sounds of
pleasure, and kicking at the dog, who is situated directly in front of him,
watching him eat. Lester stands at the window looking at field behind the
house.

LESTER'S FATHER
We got a chore needs attention.

His father puts the plate of food on a TV tray and rises from his chair.
He goes to his bed, gets down on his knees, and slides a box from underneath.

The dog knocks the fork off the plate and licks it, pushing it across the
room with its tongue.

The old man opens the box with his penknive. Inside, wrapped in thick,
clear plastic, are Larry's charred bones and skull.

LESTER'S FATHER
There's a list there for the store.

Lester picks ups a scrap of brown paper, a list of supplies scrawled on it.

EXT. RAMSEUR MAIN STREET -- LESTER & CHANCE
Lester drives down Main Street in the rusted-out Olds.

INT. PET STORE -- LESTER AND CHANCE
They walk through the bright, modern store. Lester buys Chance a
colorful toy. The other people and their dogs steer clear of them.

EXT. HARDWARE/LUMBER YARD -- LESTER AND CHANCE
Lester pulls into the lumber yard and gets out of his car. SAMSON
watches him, and sees the dog with the colorful toy in its mouth.

INT. HARDWARE--LESTER, LUCY, BETTY
Lester enters and begins looking for something. Betty and Lucy watch
him as he wanders around.

BETTY
What are you looking for?

Lester picks up a hammer, examines it, then takes the list from a pocket.

BETTY Cont'd
Is this what you want? I see you need some
wood, too.

She begins collecting what he needs.

EXT. LUMBER YARD -- SAMSON AND CHANCE
Chance is looking out the window of the car because he has dropped his
new toy. An F-150 pulls up. It is driven by a Mexican construction worker
named BALDO. A handsome young man named COOPER gets out and
goes inside. Baldo watches as Samson cautiously approaches the pit bull.

BALDO
That dog is one bad hombre. You be careful.

Samson picks up Chance's toy and gives it back to him. Then he reaches
in and gets the car keys. He opens the trunk to load the wood.

Lucy walks to the doorway and sees Lester's car in the lumber yard.

INT. HARDWARE STORE -- LUCY & LESTER
Lester walks to the checkout, where Lucy is waiting for him.

LUCY
Is that your car?

LESTER

Umm. You got some Juicy Fruit chewing gum
hiding around here?

LUCY

Juicy Fruit? No, I don't think so. Samson's
already loaded your wood.

She rings up the purchase. COOPER enters. Lucy walks around the
counter to assist him.

LUCY

You finding everything?

COOPER

I think so. Do you have some solder?

LUCY

For copper? It's right here. You'll need some
flux, too.

She takes a coil of solder off the shelf, and a tin of flux. He carries some
lengths of copper pipe, a propane torch and other supplies to the counter.
He hands her a company credit card. Lucy looks at it, then at him ...

LUCY

You work for my uncle Todd? How come I never
heard of you? What's your name?

COOPER

Cooper.

LUCY

Cooper huh. You do plumbing?

COOPER

How'd you guess? (he smiles, takes his receipt)
Thanks. (pausing at the door) What's your
name?

LUCY

Lucy.

COOPER

See ya, Lucy.

EXT. HOLLIS HOUSE -- LESTER & HIS FATHER & CHANCE
Lester is digging a grave in the backyard and his father is building a coffin about the same size as the cardboard box Larry's bones came home in.

He dumps the bones from the cardboard box into the freshly made one. When he turns his back, Chance grabs one of Larry's bones and runs into the woods. Too old and too tired to care, the father shakes his head.

EXT. BACK YARD -- LESTER & HIS FATHER & CHANCE
Lester covers the box coffin with dirt. The father looks sad and defeated.

> **LESTER**
> You want to speak over the grave?

> **LESTER'S FATHER**
> Naw. Do you?

> **LESTER**
> Naw.

> **LESTER'S FATHER**
> **(just before turning away)**
> G'bye son.

Chance, protecting his bone, watches from the woods.

EXT. COUNTY FARM -- NIGHT
It's a quiet night, the inmates are asleep.

INT. COUNTY FARM BUNKHOUSE -- RAY & OTHER INMATES
Ray is sleeping, some of the men are snoring. The INMATE whose mother sent Ray money approaches in the dark and stabs Ray with a shiv. Ray's scream echoes through the bunkhouse.

EXT. THE INFERNO -- OLDSMOBILE -- NIGHT
Lester's Olds is parked in the parking lot of The Inferno. Chance is sleeping like a baby on the backseat.

INT. INFERNO -- LUCY AND CROWD -- SAME TIME
Lucy is there with STUMP, who wants to believe he's her boyfriend. CARLA and CODY are there, too. Everybody is drinking and dancing when LESTER walks in. He sits at the bar and orders a beer. He looks around until he locates Lucy.

> **CARLA**
> Somebody's eyeballin' you.

Lucy turns to look.

                              LUCY
        Oh my god.

Stump glares at Lester.

COOPER enters The Inferno.

                              CARLA
        You see what I see?

                              LUCY
        Um-hm.

Lucy walks over and starts talking to Cooper while Carla observes. Stump
walks up to Carla.

                              STUMP
        Who's that guy?

                              CARLA
        Ya got me.

Lucy returns. Ignoring Stump, she speaks to Carla.

                              LUCY
        He wants us to come to a party later.

                              CARLA
        A party? Alright.

                              LUCY
        Come on, I'm starving.

INT. SUZIE'S DINER -- LUCY AND CARLA -- LATER
Suzie, the owner of the diner, waits on Lucy and Carla, and overhears
their conversation.

                              CARLA
        Sometimes I feel trapped in this town.

                              LUCY
        We aren't trapped, Carla. We're just stuck in our
        complacency.

                              CARLA
        Complacency? I've never heard you use that
        word before.

Suzie sits down beside Lucy.

> **SUZIE**
> I want to give you girls a little advice.

> **LUCY**
> Okay.

> **SUZIE**
> I always wanted to be a singer, I mean a professional singer, but when I was a young girl, I was afraid of pursuing it.

> **LUCY**
> Afraid? Why were you afraid?

> **SUZIE**
> I was afraid I wasn't good enough. Fear like that is a terrible thing. Promise me you won't be afraid ... (balling her fists) to catch life by the tail.

Lucy and Carla are taken aback but appreciative of this sudden speech from Suzie. They seem to take it to heart.

> **LUCY AND CARLA**
> We promise.

INT. INFERNO -- STUMP AND CODY -- SAME TIME
STUMP enters through the front door with CODY and TWO OTHER FRIENDS. They approach Lester, effectively surrounding him. Lester looks bewildered.

> **BARTENDER**
> What's going on? Take it outside.

> **STUMP**
> You heard him, let's take it outside.

Stump grabs Lester by the collar and jerks him off the stool.

EXT. INFERNO PARKING LOT -- THE BEAT DOWN
Stump lights a cigarette while CODY and two other boys keep picking on Lester. CODY punches Lester in the stomach, he doubles over. When he raises up, struggling to get his breath, there is frightening anger in his eyes and he fights them with a strength that's surprising. Eventually, they

knock him to the ground and while he's lying there he snaps his fingers. Chance goes beserk struggling to get out of Lester's car, where he's chained down. The four young men beat Lesster until he is bleeding from the nose, mouth and other places.

COOPER walks into the parking lot, pushes past Stump, CODY and the other two young men and helps Lester to his feet. LUCY and CARLA walk over from the diner to see what's happening.

COOPER
(to Lucy and Carla)
Are these guys friends of yours?

LUCY

No, huh-uh.

Whereas Lucy is quick to disassociate herself from Stump and CODY, Carla just goes along with her.

COOPER

We need to get this guy to the hospital.

Lester's car rocks with the dog's ferocious movements, trying to break his chain. He has shredded the leather upholstery.

INT. COOPER'S CAR -- LUCY, LESTER & COOPER
Lester is in the backseat with his head in Lucy's lap. He looks up at her from time to time on the way to the hospital. She strokes his cheek.

COOPER

How's he doing?

LUCY

Okay, I think. But he's still bleeding.

EXT. HOSPITAL -- LATER
A modest little hospital serving the county. COOPER and LUCY exit the emergency room. Carla, in her Mustang, is waiting in the parking lot. She honks at them.

CARLA

Where's this party you were talking about?

EXT. COOPER'S TRAILER -- PARTY -- LATER
The party is a fiesta with his Mexican co-workers. Fiesta music is playing, lights have been strung up, and their F-150's have been parked in a row. They sit in lawn chairs around a flaming firepit.

LUCY

This is some party.

CARLA

There's nothing but Mexican guys here. Where
are all the women?

COOPER

They're back in Mexico.

Lucy and Carla drink and dance with the men.

INT. HOSPITAL -- SHERIFF -- SAME NIGHT
He walks down the hallway, looking for a particular room, enters it.

INT. LESTER'S HOSPITAL ROOM -- LESTER & SHERIFF
Lester is in bed, his head and face bandaged, blood soaking through
white gauze. Sheriff Clancy walks to the bed, peers down at him. Since
Lester is unconscious, or asleep, the Sheriff can snoop around.

NEW ANGLE ON THE SHERIFF
He opens the doors of a wardrobe, sees Lester's jeans, reaches and finds
his wallet, opens it, looks at his driver's license. Returns the wallet and
finds Lester's car keys.

EXT. THE INFERNO -- SHERIFF, RALEIGH, ERNIE -- MORNING
Lester's Oldsmobile is being towed by Ernie the tow man and Deputy
Raleigh. The window of the car is broken. Chance is nowhere to be seen.
Sheriff Clancy pulls up, gets out, motions to the tow truck driver.

SHERIFF

Wait up, Ernie.

He opens Lester's car door. Raleigh steps up beside him.

RALEIGH

Holy cow.

The seats have been torn into a million little bits of leather and foam.
The Sheriff tries the key in the ignition. It fits.

SHERIFF

I thought so.

He gets out of the car, motions to Ernie ...

SHERIFF
Okay, go ahead.

THE CAMERA MOVES IN TO A CLOSE-UP OF THE BROKEN
CAR WINDOW

EXT. PORCH OF HOUSE -- CHANCE -- THAT MORNING
Lester's pit bull walks onto the porch where a small terrier is eating from
a bowl and helps himself to the tiny dog's food. The terrier growls but
Chance ignores it.

INT. THE INFERNO -- BARTENDER & SHERIFF -- SAME TIME
Ben, the bartender, pours the Sheriff a cold brew and they talk.

INT. TODD & JANEY'S HOUSE -- LUCY & JANEY -- LATER
Lucy comes home in her hardware uniform. Janey is in the kitchen
making dinner. Lucy speaks in passing ...

LUCY
Hey.

JANEY
Hey.

INT. DEN -- TODD -- AS LUCY POPS IN
Todd is practicing guitar. Lucy sits across from him.

LUCY
Sounds good.

Todd starts to sing and Lucy joins in. Carrying a dishcloth, Janey walks
to the door of the den and just watches. Lucy has a nice voice and really
gets into the song. Lucy notices Janey, perceives her look as disapproving,
and stops singing. Lucy exits the room and Todd stops playing.

TODD
What's wrong?

INT. GUEST BEDROOM -- LUCY & JANEY -- A MOMENT LATER
Lucy is taking off her work clothes with the door wide open, when Janey
enters, closes the door.

JANEY
If you don't mind. There's a man in the house,
and he happens to be my husband.

31

Janey slams the bedroom door. Then, as she walks by the den, fuming, she rolls her eyes at Todd and slaps her knee with the dish cloth.

EXT. LUMBER YARD -- SAMSON AND LUCY -- DAY
Lucy is having a bottle of pop with Samson, who has already worked up a sweat. She pulls some money out of her pocket, hands it to him.

> ### SAMSON
> What's that for?

> ### LUCY
> It's for you, go on, just take it.

> ### SAMSON
> Where'd it come from?

> ### LUCY
> I saved it up. Here.

Betty stands in the doorway of the store, watching them.

INT. HARDWARE STORE -- MR. GRAHAM & LUCY -- LATER
BETTY stands nearby and SAMSON stands in the doorway.

> ### LUCY
> I swear on God's holy Bible I did not steal any-thing. Why would you think that?

> ### MR. GRAHAM
> There's a hundred dollars missing from the regis-ter. Lucy, don't play me for an idiot.

FLASHBACK TO BETTY (JUST A FEW MINUTES EARLIER)
Alone behind the cash register, she takes five twenties from the till and puts them in her purse while Lucy is outside talking to Samson.

BACK TO SCENE WITH EVERYONE
Samson holds up the money Lucy gave him. Mr. Graham snatches it from him.

> ### SAMSON
> I'm sorry Mr. Graham.

MR. GRAMHAM

There's only forty-eight dollars here, where's the rest of it?

LUCY

That's my money, I swear it is.

MR. GRAHAM

Go on and get your things Lucy. You're fired. *(to Samson)* You, too. Go on, get out of here.

Betty is pleased with herself.

EXT. TODD AND JANEY'S HOUSE -- LATER THAT DAY

Lucy is sitting in the swingset, drinking a beer, when Janey comes home. Janey stops at the edge of the parking area, hand on hip.

JANEY

I heard you got canned. And that nice black man whose wife has cancer.

LUCY

So?

JANEY

So? So, I guess we aren't gonna get any help with the rent are we?

Janey goes inside.

CUT TO TODD AND SHERIFF CLANCY

Coming across the adjacent pasture in an ATV, a dead deer across the back of it. They stop at a tree at the edge of the yard.

NEW ANGLE -- LUCY, TODD AND SHERIFF

Lucy walks over as they string up the deer for processing, using a spreader. The deer has already been field dressed.

LUCY

Who shot it?

SHERIFF

Toddy did. Right there ...

He points to a little hole in the deer's neck.

TODD

Lucy, honey, will you run grab us some coolers.

Lucy walks inside.

INT. KITCHEN -- LUCY AND JANEY -- SAME TIME

LUCY

They need some coolers, Toddy says.

JANEY

I am sick to my ears of eating deer meat. The coolers are in the pantry.

Lucy drags two coolers out of the pantry,

JANEY

Make sure he washes the blood and shit off real good.

LUCY

Okay.

BACK TO THE DEER SKINNING SCENE

Lucy brings them the coolers. Working in tandem, Todd and Sheriff Clancy have most of the skin off. Lucy sits nearby and watches. JANEY comes out of the house with three cold beers. She opens a beer for Todd, Sheriff Clancy, and one for herself. She hands a beer to each man, who accept them with bloody hands. The Sheriff's cell phone rings.

SHERIFF

Would one of you answer that for me.

He steps over so that either Janey or Lucy can get his cell phone out of his pants pocket. Lucy gets there first.

LUCY

Hello? He's here, but he's cuttin' up a deer at the moment. Oh really? Wow. Okay, I'll tell him.

She flips the phone shut.

LUCY

Okay, she said ... that was Sarah... and she said there was an accident out twenty-nine east of the Trinity overpass and you should get over there ASAP. The firemen are gonna use the *jaws of life*.

SHERIFF

Hmm. Sorry Todd.

TODD

Hey, no problem. I'll finish this up.

SHERIFF

There's always some numbskull having an accident to disrupt my day off. Never fails.

EXT. HIGHWAY -- SHERIFF -- LATER

With the accident cleared up, the Sheriff gets in his car and answers the
radio.

SHERIFF

What is it Sarah?

SARAH

Ray Speckle is being transferred to Memorial

SHERIFF

You're kidding me. When?

SARAH

Tonight.

SHERIFF

Tell Raleigh to meet me over there.

SARAH

Copy that.

INT. HOSPITAL--RAY AND LESTER -- SAME DAY

The hospital is silent except for a nurse doing paperwork at a well-lit
station when RAY SPECKLE is wheeled on a gurney down the hallway
by two prison guards.

When they pass LESTER's room, he sees them. He gets a glimpse of
Ray -- curious, he gets out of bed and walks to Ray's door. Lester's head
is partially bandaged. A nurse walks past. Lester watches the guards
interact with the nurse outside Ray's room, and overhears them ...

GUARD ONE

The Sheriff will be sending over someone to
guard him. He's not going to be any trouble.
He's that televangelist.

GUARD TWO

He's on a heavy tranquilizer.

Later, Lester leaves his room. Ray is sweating profusely, sleeping fitfully, when Lester enters the room and walks to his bedside. Lester sees Ray's Bible beside the bed and his name **Ray Speckle, Pastor** imprinted in gold letters. Ray groans and reaches out one hand like a man trying to find his way in the dark. Lester, seeing a glass of water on the tray near Ray's bed, holds the glass out for him, but of course Ray is half-asleep, so Lester puts the glass to his lips. Ray takes a sip and calms down.

CUT TO HALLWAY -- SHERIFF CLANCY
He's coming to see Ray.

BACK IN RAY'S ROOM -- RAY, LESTER AND THE SHERIFF
Lester is hiding in the wardrobe when the Sheriff enters. While Lester watches, the Sheriff leans over Ray.

> **SHERIFF**
> I'm telling ya Ray, you're gonna owe me for this.

Sheriff Clancy looks up. RALEIGH stands at the door to Ray's room.

> **SHERIFF**
> You up to standing guard tonight?

> **RALEIGH**
> Sure, that's why I got out of bed and strapped
> my holster on. So I could watch a sick fella sleep.

INT. TODD AND JANEY'S HOUSE -- LUCY -- SAME NIGHT
Lucy, in a rather revealing pajama outfit -- short shorts and camisole -- walks down the hallway to the closed door of Todd and Janey's bedroom, a wad of money in her hand. She knocks.

> **JANEY (O.S.)**
> Who is it?

> **LUCY**
> It's me. Lucy.

> **JANEY**
> What do you want?

> **LUCY**
> I want to give you something.

> **JANEY**
> Come on in.

Lucy opens the door.

NEW ANGLE -- TODD, JANEY AND LUCY
It's obvious that Todd and Janey have been making love.

> **LUCY**
> Did I come in at a bad time?

> **JANEY**
> What do you want, Lucy?

Lucy drops the money on their bed.

> **LUCY**
> There. That's all I have.

> **TODD**
> We don't care about your money, Lucy.

> **JANEY**
> Yes we do.

> **TODD**
> I mean, we care, because it's a good thing when
> you pitch in.

Janey gets up to find a cigarette, while Lucy lingers.

> **JANEY**
> What is it now?

> **LUCY**
> I'm leaving here.

> **JANEY**
> Leaving? Now there's an idea.

> **LUCY**
> I gotta catch my own life by the tail sometime.
> Like tomorrow maybe.

> **JANEY**
> Well, good luck darlin'.

Lucy exits.

TODD
(opening the covers)
Get in here.

INT. RAY'S HOSPITAL ROOM -- THAT NIGHT
RALEIGH is asleep in a chair in RAY's room. LESTER slips out of the
wardrobe and out of the room.

EXT. ANIMAL SHELTER -- LESTER'S CAR -- NEXT DAY
Lester's car is in the parking lot.

INT. ANIMAL SHELTER -- LESTER & DESK LADY -- SAME TIME

DESK LADY
A pit bull?

Lester nods.

DESK LADY
Okay. Well, we had one brought in, a male dog,
brown. Sound like your dog?

LESTER
Yes ma'am.

DESK LADY
Unfortunately, we had to put him down.

LESTER
You put him down?

DESK LADY
Yes. He had killed a number of local pets and
when we got him he was unmanageable.

LESTER
Down where?

DESK LADY
Down ... as in *dead.*

Surprise crosses Lester's face, then sadness. He turns solemnly to exit.

DESK LADY
Sir? Is this yours?

She holds up a big dog collar. Lester looks at it, takes it gently.

CLOSE-UP OF THE COLLAR
A handmade leather collar, engraved with a cowboy design motif, and the name "Chance."

EXT. ANIMAL SHELTER -- LESTER & CAR -- SAME TIME
When Lester gets to his car, he releases his anger by pounding hard on the hood, sending up a cloud of rust dust.

INT. LUCY'S BEDROOM -- LUCY -- MORNING
Lucy wakes up, rubs her eyes. Lucy talks to herself ...

LUCY
This is the first day of the rest of my life. The first day of the rest of my life.

A minute later, she has opened her purse and found two dollars.

LUCY
I have two dollars, so I've got *some* money.

A minute later, she has pulled a sweatshirt over her head.

LUCY
I don't really have a good reason to leave.

A minute later, she is tying the shoestrings on her sneakers.

LUCY
I don't really have a good reason to stay.

She hears church bells and steps toward the window. Then she bolts out of the room.

INT. KITCHEN -- TODD AND LUCY -- SAME TIME
Todd is seated at the kitchen table, reading the newspaper.

LUCY
It's Sunday!

TODD
That's probably why Janey is at church.

LUCY
Why aren't you with her?

TODD
Because I have a newspaper to read.

LUCY
Can I borrow your truck then?

TODD
Why do you need the truck?

LUCY
I want to go to church, too.

EXT. COOPER'S TRAILER -- LUCY AND COOPER
Lucy, dressed for church, pulls up in Todd's truck, hops out and goes to the door, knocks. Baldo and some of the other Mexican guys watch her.

BALDO
Ola Lucy.

COOPER opens the door of the trailer.

LUCY
You got any church clothes?

EXT. BAPTIST CHURCH -- LATER
A pretty little church in the country.

INT. BAPTIST CHURCH -- SAME TIME
The choir is singing when LUCY and COOPER walk in. This is SAMSON's church and they find him sitting with his family on the third row. They slip into the pew. The children wave at Lucy and she waves back.

EXT. CHURCH PICNIC -- RIVER-SIDE -- LATER
The church is having a picnic at a park beside a river, a softball field and horseshoe pits are nearby, and the old men are already pitching shoes while the women are setting out the food on tables. Before the meal starts, everyone holds hands and the pastor says a prayer. Then they dig in. Cooper seems to be enjoying himself. Samson is there with his family and so is Harold, the cook at Suzie's Diner. We overhear some people talking.

WOMAN ONE
That's the Speckle girl. She killed that boy.

They look at Lucy and Cooper, who are sitting down with their plates of food.

WOMAN ONE Cont'd
She stabbed him through the heart. I mean, that was something brutal wasn't it.

WOMAN TWO
Um-hm, it sure was. And look at her now, she's got a new fella.

WOMAN THREE
I say, she's got herself a good lookin' boy.

While the PASTOR eats he is talking to several men.

PASTOR
I don't think our Becky is going to survive the chemo.

MAN ONE
You don't say. That happens sometimes.

They glance over at Samson. Becky is leaning against him and their daughter is helping her eat.

MAN TWO
How's our boy holding up?

PASTOR
He's bearing his cross alright, from what I see.

EXT. PARK -- THE PICNIC
Kids are playing softball, old men are pitching horseshoes.

EXT. RIVER AT THE PARK -- LUCY AND COOPER
They walk along together.

LUCY
Last night I told my aunt and uncle I was leaving today.

COOPER
Why'd you say that?

LUCY
Because I hate this town.

COOPER
Hate it? Really? You hate all those people over there?

LUCY
No, I don't hate *them.*

COOPER
The Mexican guys that work for Todd, they'd give a testicle for what we have.

LUCY
But I'm *me,* and I don't see me having much of a future here. If I had one good reason to stay, I would, but honest-to-God, I can't think of one.

Cooper pulls her to him and kisses her.

LUCY
Is that supposed to ...

He kisses her again, this time it's a longer, passionate kiss.

EXT. SUZIE'S DINER -- LUCY -- NEXT DAY
The day is bright, cheery. Lucy walks down the sidewalk to the diner.

INT. DINER -- LUCY, SUZIE & HAROLD
The breakfast crowd has thinned out. Harold is in the kitchen and Suzie is pouring herself coffee. Val and Gloria, the other waitresses, are bussing tables and doing other chores. Lucy walks in. She sits at the counter.

SUZIE
Harold tells me you're lookin' for work.

LUCY
Yes ma'am.

Harold, the cook, observes them from the kitchen.

SUZIE
Waitressing is hard work, contrary to what some people think. It's especially hard on your arches. Do you have good arches?

42

LUCY
Yes ma'am, far as I know, I do.

She drops a clean apron on the counter in front of her.

Harold comes from the kitchen. Lucy is tying the apron on. Harold picks up a Polaroid camera from underneath the front counter.

HAROLD
Smile.

He snaps a picture and hands it to Lucy.

HAROLD
(referring to the photo)
Stick it up there when all the colors come up.

He motions to a place on the wall where Polaroids of all the employees are thumbtacked up.

INT. APARTMENT -- SUZIE AND LUCY -- LATER
Suzie opens the door and they enter. Lucy looks around.

LUCY
I didn't expect this.

SUZIE
Well, I'd just as soon rent it to an employee, so long as you won't tear up anything.

LUCY
I won't tear it up. It's nice.

SUZIE
Yes it is. Because I only rent to nice people.

Lucy smiles.

SUZIE
Us single girls have to take of ourselves, don't we.

LUCY
Yes ma'am. Suzie, this is a real blessing on my head.

                          SUZIE
        Well, here ya go.

She drops the apartment key into Lucy's hand.

EXT. TODD AND JANEY'S HOUSE -- JANEY & RAY
Janey and Ray pull up in the Bronco and get out. She puts her arm
through his as they walk to the door. He is weak from his infection and
his ribs have not totally healed.

INT. KITCHEN -- JANEY AND RAY -- LATER
Janey is making pancakes.

                          RAY
        When I was inside, I dreamed about your pan-
        cakes.

                         JANEY
        Really? I didn't know you liked my cooking all
        that much.

                          RAY
        Inside you have time to think about pancakes.
Janey puts a plate of pancakes and bacon in front of him.

                         JANEY
        I can't believe you had to go to jail just for pro-
        tecting your own flesh and blood.

                          RAY
        They should never put a man in a cage, I don't
        care what he's done. If he's done truly bad, be
        merciful, kill him. Life in a cage is no life at all.

                         JANEY
        You got any plans?

                          RAY
        I got all kinds of plans, sis. First off, I plan to eat
        some pancakes.

INT. CLOSET -- RAY -- LATER
Darkness -- until Ray opens the closet and retrieves a cowboy shirt, silky
black with white piping and pearl snaps.

                            44

INT. RAY'S BEDROOM -- RAY

In front of the mirror, he slides into the shirt then slips a bolo tie around his neck. The bolo tie features a large polished stone. He puts on a black Stetson. TODD walks in.

TODD

Hey brother-in-law.

Ray turns, steps toward Todd, hugs him a little too hard. Ray winces.

TODD

Good to see ya, fella. Oh, sorry.

RAY

Good to see you, Toddy boy.

TODD

You're lookin' sharp. Goin' out?

RAY

Thought I might wet my whistle. You know how that goes.

TODD

Yes I do. Hey, me n' the boys are playin' The Inferno. Why don't you come along?

RAY

I'd appreciate that.

TODD

Okay then.

RAY

I think I'll just sit here for awhile, til you're ready.

TODD

That'll be fine.

Todd leaves. Ray sits down and takes his Bible in hand, opens it and begins to read. A moment passes before Todd pops back in. He's putting on a fancy shirt.

                              TODD
You talk to Lucy yet?

                              RAY
No, not yet.

                              TODD
Okay. Well. She works over at Suzie's. You know
Suzie.

                              RAY
Yes, I know Suzie.

                              TODD
Okay, well ...

He walks away, still talking:

                          TODD (O.S.)
I'm sure she'd like to see you.

INT. THE INFERNO -- THAT EVENING
Todd's band is cranked up. Ray sits at the bar, drinking a beer. He's all
dressed up, out of place, but happy. He looks around, watches the band,
smiles a little smile.

LUCY and CARLA enter with STUMP AND CODY. Ray stands when
he sees his daughter, steps toward her, and they embrace. He clings to
her for a long time and she begins to notice that her friends are staring.
She gently wiggles out of his embrace, and they sit down at a table across
from each other.

                              LUCY
I heard you was shivved in prison.

                              RAY
I was. And it hurt.

                              LUCY
But you're okay now, right?

                              RAY
Sweetness, I am a changed man. In county I
took sick from the filthy knife plunged into my
ribs, and I had a fever dream and in this fever
dream I saw the whole world on fire. And I was
in the fire, and your sweet heavenly mother ...

                               46

LUCY

Momma was there?

RAY

Yes. She came forth with a cool drink of water.

LUCY

Was I there?

RAY

No, darling, you were spared.

COOPER enters. He sees Lucy and Ray talking.

LUCY

You got some money?

RAY

Enough for tonight.

LUCY

You look good, dad.

He touches her shiny red hair.

RAY

So do you pun'kin.

LUCY

Daddy, please don't call me that.

RAY

Okay sweetness. (beat) Nobody's been askin'
questions or anything?

LUCY

No. (beat) I'm here with friends.

Ray glances up at Carla, Stump and Cody.

RAY

I'm just gonna drink.

LUCY

Okay pops.

She kisses him on the forehead and walks away.

LUCY
Good to have you home.

Lucy walks up beside Cooper near the stage. Todd's band is at the pinnacle of a hard-rocking song. Lucy sways, drinks from her bottle of beer.

EXT. LUCY'S APARTMENT -- MORNING
Another hot day, a slight breeze.

INT. APARTMENT -- LUCY AND COOPER
Lucy is making breakfast. Cooper is getting dressed. The rumpled bed in the background makes it obvious they spent the night together.

LUCY
We shouldn't done what we did. It was the beer.
We're just stupid I guess.

COOPER
Then let's be stupid some more, Lucy.

He picks her up, spatula in hand, and carries her back to the bedroom.

LUCY
Stop it, the eggs'll burn!

He tickles her and she laughs.

EXT. TODD AND JANEY'S HOUSE -- RAY -- LATER
Ray, dressed to impress, as usual, walks out the back door into the yard. He carries his big black Bible. He sets the Bible down. Under a tarp, he finds an old scooter. He opens the gas tank, sticks a finger in, smells it. He rolls it away from the house, brushes off the seat, gets on, cranks it, rides down the driveway ... then he turns around.

CUT TO A FEW MINUTES LATER -- RAY
Bible lashed onto the scooter's rear rack, he rides away.

INT. SUZIE'S CAFE -- SUZIE, VAL, GLORIA & LUCY -- LATER
Suzie, Val and Gloria are busy preparing for lunch.

SUZIE
You're late.

NEW ANGLE, WIDER TO INCLUDE LUCY
As she puts her purse away and flings on an apron.

LUCY

I know. I'm sorry.

SUZIE

I'm sorry won't cut the lettuce and tomatoes.

LUCY

I know. I'm a bad person.

ANGLES ON VAL AND GLORIA
Val winks at Lucy to break the tension. During Suzie's next spiel, Gloria
makes a yak-yak motion with her hand.

SUZIE

Honey, I'd've thought you had a drug addiction,
or a boy addiction, or a life controlling issue of
any kind ... I would never have hired you.

A customer -- LESTER -- walks in and sits down.

VAL
(to Lester)

Hon, we'll be right with you.

SUZIE
(referring to Lester)

You want to help him?

Lucy walks toward Lester. -- she recognizes him, she thinks -- she slows
down, gets a second look, approaches cautiously ...

LUCY

Hey there. You ready to order something?

LESTER

Chicken n' taters n' a side of coleslaw.

LUCY

Okay. How 'bout some tea?

LESTER

Some tea what to choke it all down. Oh, and
everwhat's good for desert.

LUCY

Peach cobbler?

                              LESTER
              That'll do.

Lucy walks away. He recollects the evening she stoked his face.

FLASHBACK TO COOPER'S CAR -- LUCY AND LESTER
Lucy strokes Lester's cheek.

BACK TO CURRENT SCENE

                              LUCY
              I'll bring you a basket of hot cornbread, how's
              that.

He smiles.

ANGLE ON LUCY AND VAL
As Lucy goes to put in Lester's order.

                              LUCY
              Oh my god, Val, he's the man they beat up at
              The Inferno a couple months ago.

She marches over to Lester's table.

                              LUCY
              I know who you are, and I'm sorry for what hap-
              pened to you.

She sits across from him.

                              LUCY
              No, I really am. Are you all better? You know,
              better. Are you feeling okay?

                             LESTER
              Ma'am, if I could get me some cornbread ...

                              LUCY
              Cornbread? Okay, sure, yeah.

NEW ANGLE ON LUCY AND SUZIE
As she gets Lester's cornbread.

                              LUCY
              Suzie, I think that boy's retarded or something.

SUZIE

He just looks a tad slow to me. His money still
spends.

CAMERA FOLLOWS LUCY TO LESTER'S TABLE
She carries a basket of cornbread, sets it in front of him. He takes a big
bite, chews, then finally looks up, his mouth full, because Lucy is stuck
there, staring at him.

LUCY

Is it good?

He nods, smiles.

LUCY

I'm glad. Your chicken will be up before long. I
better run check.

She walks away.

LESTER

Ma'am. That fella what helped me, him a good
man. And you purdy. A real purdy person.

Lester takes another huge bite of cornbread.

Dressed right and clutching his Bible, Ray Speckle enters and finds a
table.

SUZIE, VAL AND GLORIA

Hi Ray.

Ray sits down as Gloria arrives at his table with a cup of coffee.

GLORIA

You doin' some street evangelism?

RAY

Not today. Too daggum hot.

CUT TO LESTER
Stealing a glance at Ray.

CUT TO LUCY
as she walks over to Ray's table.

LUCY

Hi pops. Did you walk all the way to town just to see me?

RAY

I didn't walk, I scootered. (beat) Why won't you come out to Janey's?

LUCY

Janey and I don't tolerate so well.

RAY

I know, and I'm sorry. Some forgiveness is due, ya reckon?

LUCY

Do you want to look at a menu?

CUT TO HAROLD, THE COOK
Poking his head in from the kitchen.

HAROLD

Lucy, you still want to run out to Samson's place?

SUZIE

We're covered here.

LUCY

Okay, if I can drive your car, Harold.

HAROLD

Oh god.

ANGLE THAT INCLUDES RAY AND LUCY

LUCY

Gotta go.

She gives him a kiss.

RAY

Come out and say hi to your Aunt Janey. Somebody's got to be the reed that bends.

LUCY

Okay. Sunday. Maybe.

RAY

I'm holding you to it, sweetness.

EXT. RURAL ROAD -- LUCY -- LATER

Lucy drives down the road in Harold's ancient Celica, spewing smoke.

INT. CAR -- CLOSE-UP OF FOOD

Tin trays of food sit on the car seat.

BACK TO SUZIE'S DINER -- SUZIE AND RAY -- SAME TIME

Suzie walks over to Ray's table.

SUZIE

How's the potato salad?

RAY

It's awfully fine.

SUZIE

You doin' okay?

RAY

Good as can be expected.

SUZIE

You know, Ray, something I always wanted to ask you is why you put so much store by Jesus.

RAY

That is a mystery to me, sugar.

SUZIE

A mystery? That's how you explain it?

RAY

It can't be explained. The name of Jesus makes my heart go weak and fluttery.

SUZIE

Fluttery huh.

RAY

Like I swallowed a hummingbird.

Lester has been listening to Ray, now he turns and looks.

RAY
Is that who I think it is?

Ray gets up and slips into the booth across the table from Lester.

RAY
It's you. From the hospital. How are you there
fella?

LESTER
I'm a holdin' both ends together still I guess.

RAY
Excellante, man-o-man, it's good to see you.

Lester almost manages a smile. Suzy just watches, shakes her head.

EXT. SAMSON'S HOUSE -- SAMSON, HIS FAMILY & LUCY
Samson's kids, including teenagers, are removing the food from the car.
Samson steps off the porch and Lucy rushes to give him a hug. Samson's
wife, Becky, sits on the porch. She smiles, but she's smiling through pain.

CUT TO FARM LAND -- LUCY AND SAMSON -- LATER
Lucy has hold of his arm as they walk down a dirt road between fields.

SAMSON
The doctor says her tumors are shrunk up to the
size of grapes.

LUCY
Grapes? That's real good I guess.

SAMSON
Yeah, it's good alright, but the doctor says it's
mastacized and has to be cut out. Only he wants
to cut her breasts off, two at once.

LUCY
Oh my god, that's horrible.

SAMSON
She'll have no more breasts at all.

LUCY
I can't imagine ...

SAMSON
I ain't tole her that part yet.

LUCY
Samson, I'm sorry all this is happening to you
n' her. We'll keep runnin' food out, much as we
can, I promise.

SAMSON
It helps to have home-cooked food.

Lucy presses her head gently against his shoulder.

EXT. JOB SITE -- LUCY, TODD, COOPER, BALDO, OTHERS
Lucy, feeling rather forlorn after visiting Samson, stops by the house that
Todd and his crew are building. Baldo and some of the other workers
wave at Lucy. Todd walks over.

TODD
Hey, everything okay?

LUCY
Yeah. I just took food out to Samson.

TODD
How's he doing?

LUCY
His wife, Becky, has breast cancer.

TODD
Damn, I hate to hear that. Fuckin' cancer.

LUCY
The house is lookin' good.

TODD
We'll have it dried in tomorrow. I guess you
came to see Cooper. There he is. Why don't you
wave.

She waves.

TODD
There, happy?

LUCY

A little.

TODD

Okay then, I'll see ya, Red.
(walking away)
Got a house waitin' on me.

INT. LUCY'S APT. BEDROOM -- LUCY & COOPER -- MORNING
Cooper is drawing on Lucy's bare back. She turns to face him.

LUCY

I used to think all men were pigs.

COOPER

Not all of us, just most of us. But not me.

LUCY

I know something like what we have can't last
forever. No, really. Balloons always burst or else
they shrivel up to little balls.

COOPER

Don't say things like that.

LUCY

Why not?

COOPER

Just don't.

Cooper stands up, puts his pants and shirt on.

COOPER

I've been wondering something. How is it you
got such a light sentence ... for ... you know ...
what you did to that guy?

LUCY

I got an involuntary manslaughter, cause he
raped me.

COOPER

And what'd your old man get?

LUCY

He got improper disposal of a body and helping
me after I did the manslaughter. And running
from law enforcement, too, I think. Satisfied?

COOPER
(chuckling to himself)

Yeah, I'm satisfied.

EXT. OLD TIRE STORE -- RAY -- ANOTHER DAY
Ray is looking at an old tire store that's for rent. The door is open and he
walks inside.

INT. TIRE STORE -- NEW ANGLE ON RAY
He walks in, looks around. Behind him, LESTER steps into the doorway.

RAY

Well if it ain't the man from the hospital his own
self. What can I do you for, friend?

He walks up to Lester.

LESTER

I come by ... I seen your scooter, so I come by.

RAY

I'm fixin' to open up a church here in this rat
trap of a former tire center. Tell me, are you a
Christian man, Lester?

LESTER

No, I ain't even looked at the book. My pappy's
got some bitterness in him way things've gone, n'
some of that spilled over I guess.

RAY

Well, that's not going to keep you from being
embraced in fellowship here. No sir, it will not.
Tell me, Lester, what's your last name?

LESTER

Chance. Lester Chance.

RAY

Lester Chance takin' a chance with Reverend
Ray ... ain't that nice. Come on ...

Lester follows Ray outside.

EXT. TIRE STORE -- NEW ANGLE -- RAY AND LESTER

>
RAY
First thing we need is a sign. Resurrection Temple.

>
LESTER
You wanna make this here tire center into a temple ... not sure you oughta do that.

>
RAY
What's your reasoning there, my friend?

>
LESTER
I ain't seen such a thing, that's all. But that's just me.

>
RAY
Look around, Lester, our God is the creator god. Surely now he can help us create a church out of this place. Unless he's too tired.

Lester doesn't get the joke.

>
LESTER
How come you want to do something like this here?

>
RAY
Build a church, you mean? Well, it's what I do.

>
LESTER
This world's a spiteful place.

>
RAY
You've seen that in a firsthand way, haven't you. The beating, I'm saying.

>
LESTER
Yessir, there's that, and my brother. He broke Daddy's heart running off to take drugs n' chase girls.

RAY

We're going to pray for your brother. That's hard
to believe. We're going to meet a holy God ...
face to face. Right here.

Lester doesn't reply but seems impressed with Ray's enthusiasm.

INT. TIRE CENTER/CHURCH -- RAY & LESTER -- LATER
They have been working hard cleaning up the place. Now they are
taking a break. Lester points at Ray's white shirt, where a blood stain has
appeared on his side.

RAY

My good shirt.

He opens his shirt and his undershirt has a wet red stain on it.

LESTER

You oughta get that looked after.

RAY

You know, the Lord Jesus was pierced in the side,
yes he was. Now I can identify, sure enough.

Lester is truly impressed. Ray presses a wad of paper towels against his
ribs, then he sits right across from Lester.

RAY

Lester, I think it's time you asked the Lord Jesus
into your heart.

He takes Lester's hand.

RAY Cont'd

You have become my friend, and a friend of
God. Helping out like you have. I think it's time
you gave your heart to Jesus, what do you say?

LESTER

If I do as you say, what difference will it make?

RAY

Oh, it will make all the difference.

NEW VIEW OF RAY AND LESTER THROUGH WINDOW
The window is cloudy and smudged but through it we see the interior of
the former tire center, and evidence of the cleaning up work done by Ray
and Lester.

Ray puts his hand on Lester's head and they appear to pray together, although Ray is doing all the the praying. They finish praying ...

> **RAY**
> Now, don't that feel good? I think we should take communion. I have these crackers. And I have this here grape Nehi.

He begins to prepare the elements.

> You do know what communion is, don't you, Lester? It's when we remember the work Jesus did on the cross.

> **LESTER**
> Where he went and died, you mean?

> **RAY**
> Yes, on that Roman cross of torture and shame. Well, let's just eat this juice and crackers. God sees to the heart of the matter. That's right. Um-hm. Yes he does.

EXT. TODD AND JANEY'S HOUSE -- LATER
Todd comes home, parks his truck.

INT. KITCHEN -- TODD AND JANEY
Janey is cooking dinner when Todd walks in.

> **JANEY**
> Hi honey.

Todd doesn't answer, marches past her to the bedroom.

> **JANEY**
> Todd?

She follows him down the hallway.

INT. BEDROOM -- TODD AND JANEY
Todd is shucking his dirty clothes.

> **JANEY**
> Honey, what's wrong? You want a beer?

He marches into the bathroom, she follows behind.

JANEY

Todd, talk to me.

He gets in the shower, turns on the water. Her hand enters frame and turns it off. He tries again. She turns it off. He flings the curtain open.

TODD

I'd like to take a shower.

JANEY

What in the world is wrong with you?

He puts a towel around his waist and sits on the commode.

TODD

Bring that beer, will ya?

She marches out to get it.

CAMERA FOLLOWS HER
Back down the hallway and into the kitchen ...

JANEY

I wish you wouldn't do this to me, you know how I hate the silent treatment, of course that's exactly why you do it, I know, and it works. But whatever it is that is causing you to act this way can't be so terrible ...

She pauses upon retrieving a beer from the fridge.

JANEY Cont'd

Unless. (beat) Honey, if this is what I think it is, I was planning to tell you, I just hadn't yet had the chance, and even if it is that it's not the end of the world, in fact, it's a good thing if you stop and think about it.

She returns to the bathroom, hands Todd the beer.

JANEY

It's a good thing.

He pops open the beer.

TODD

What is?

61

JANEY
Whatever it is that has you so concerned.

TODD
Jeremy Ingles from the bank dropped by the job
site. He wanted me to know that you withdrew
two thousand dollars from our savings account.

JANEY
That little turd.

TODD
It was for Ray, for his new church, right?
But two friggin' thousand?

JANEY
I invested it in a kingdom project.

TODD
No, Janey, you blew it on a Ray Speckle project.
Now, I'm going to take a shower. If you don't
mind.

He stands, drops the towel with a flourish, and beer in hand steps into the
shower.

INT. KITCHEN -- TODD, JANEY & RAY -- LATER
Ray and Janey are already sitting at the kitchen table, which is spread
with food, when Todd enters wearing clean clothes, hair still wet. He sits
without speaking.

TODD
I have a lot of lumber and other materials in
storage. You can use it for your church.

Janey looks at Todd and smiles.

EXT. PORCH OF HOUSE -- RAY -- LATER
Ray sits on the porch swing, beer in hand, listening to Janey play a hymn
inside on the piano. The house windows spill yellow light onto the porch.

CUT TO JANEY PLAYING THE PIANO

CLOSE-UP OF RAY
Singing along, eyes closed, blissful.

NEW ANGLE ON TODD
As he steps onto the porch and pops open a beer.

BACK TO RAY
He slowly opens one eye.

SCENE WITH TODD AND RAY

TODD
I don't appreciate you going to Janey for money
behind my back. She's weak when it comes to
you, and you know that. (beat) You need to move
on, Ray. Yeah. I think that would be best.

INT. HARDWARE STORE -- LESTER -- THAT MORNING
Lester walks the aisles looking at paint.

LESTER'S P.O.V. --- CANS OF PAINT
He sees double images of the cans, but he picks up a few anyway.

NEW ANGLE ON LESTER AND BETTY AT CHECK-OUT
Lester puts three gallons of paint on the counter.

BETTY
Looks like somebody's going to do some painting
today.

LESTER
What color's that can there?

BETTY
Well, that's white, those two cans, and that can is
red. Is that what you wanted?

Lester nods.

EXT. SUZIE'S CAFE -- RAY -- SAME TIME
Ray, wearing cool shades, pulls up on his scooter.

INT. SUZIE'S CAFE -- VAL, HAROLD & RAY
Ray enters. He's the first customer as its early morning. He sits down. Val
hands him a cup of coffee. Harold, in the kitchen, steals a glance at Ray.

RAY
Is Suzie around?

VAL
She's taking the day off.

                              RAY
        Day off huh?

                              VAL
        That's right.

His hand shaking, Ray takes a bottle of bourbon out of his satchel and
pours some into his coffee.

ANGLE ON VAL
Watching him. She shakes her head.

                              VAL
                          (to Harold)
        It's not everyday you see a preacher do that.

INT. LUCY'S APARTMENT -- LUCY & COOPER -- SAME TIME
Lucy is still asleep, Cooper is quietly dressing. He sneaks out.

EXT. SUZIE'S HOUSE -- RAY AND SUZIE -- THAT MORNING
Suzie is busy working in her flower garden when Ray pulls up on his
scooter.

                             SUZIE
        Ray, what are you doing here?

                              RAY
        I don't know. Thought I'd pay you a visit.

                             SUZIE
        You want me to make coffee?

                              RAY
                       (removing his sunglasses)
        Nah, I'm good.

                             SUZIE
        So what's going on with you?

                              RAY
        Well, I'll tell ya. I've decided to move out of
        Janey's place. I was thinkin'...

                               64

SUZIE

Don't think, Ray, don't think. Honey our little fling-a-ding is ancient history. We can't go back there. You can't move in here. Sorry.

Ray gets on his scooter, puts his sunglasses back on, and drives away.

EXT. HAWKINS LAKE -- LUCY & COOPER -- LATE MORNING
They have been swimming and now stretch out on towels warmed by the sun. The water shines golden, as if on fire.

LUCY

You know what my daddy says? He says people today are swimming in a lake of fire.

COOPER

A lake of fire, huh, like the one in Revelation?

LUCY

You know the Bible pretty good.

COOPER

Just the judgement parts. That's what my father liked to remind me of ... the eternal hell I was headed for.

LUCY

You're a good man.

COOPER

Not that good.

Cooper is flat on his back. Lucy reaches over and traces the ridge of his nose with her index finger.

LUCY

I like your nose. (beat) Coop?

COOPER

Yeah?

LUCY

You are the best thing to ever happen in my life.

EXT. TIRE STORE -- LESTER AND RAY -- LATER
Lester is standing in front of the tire store, paint can and brush in hand
when Ray pulls up on his scooter. Ray walks to where Lester is standing
and looks up at the big sign Lester has painted. It reads: Rezeewreckshun
Tempul in atrocious hand-painted letters. Ray reaches for his bottle of
bourbon, slips it from his satchel, but simply holds it at his side.

> **RAY**
> Son, we're gonna have to get you checked.
> That's not even close.

Ray steps in front of Lester and scrutinizes his face. Without removing
his sunglasses, he drinks from the bottle.

> **RAY**
> Don't you think God expects our dead level best?
> Is that your dead level best?

Lester nods.

> **RAY**
> Well, I expect it is. But its not up to the heavenly
> standard, son. It's just not.

Lester puts the paint down and goes to his Olds, bangs on the roof, dust
flying, gets in and drives away. Ray takes another swig of bourbon.

EXT. BALL FIELD -- JANEY, TODD & TEAMS -- THAT NIGHT
Todd is playing softball. Shortstop. His team is in the field when Janey
arrives. She walks straight onto the field.

> **JANEY**
> Ray got himself arrested.

> **TODD**
> So?

> **JANEY**
> So we have to post his bail.

> **TODD**
> No we don't. Go ahead and pitch, Leroy.

LEROY

You sure?

TODD

I'm sure. Don't mind her. Go ahead. Else we'll
be here all night. I know how stubborn she is.

JANEY

We are too going to post his bail.

Janey stands in front of him. He has to move side-to-side to see the batter.

TODD

Why should we?

JANEY

Because he's flesh and blood.

TODD

He's your no count crazy Primitive Baptist
brother is what he is.

The batter hits a grounder right at Janey. She jumps, Todd snags the ball
and throws the runner out at first. It's the last out and Todd's team heads
to the dugout. Janey follows him.

JANEY

He ran over that old Pruitt woman's cat.

TODD

He did what?

JANEY

He ran over her cat with his motorcyle.

TODD

Is it dead?

JANEY

Yes it's dead. The old lady's pressing charges.

EDDIE

Todd, you're up, dude.

Todd walks out of the dugout and takes some practice swings. Janey stays in the dugout talking to him through the fence.

> **TODD**
> **(pauses, thinking)**
> How the hell did he run over a cat?

> **JANEY**
> He was drunk.

> **TODD**
> Surprise. You know he's an alcoholic.

Janey rolls her eyes and makes a face like she doesn't want anyone to hear that particular piece of dirty laundry.

> **TODD**
> How much is bail?

> **JANEY**
> Five hundred.

> **TODD**
> No way.

> **JANEY**
> Todd.

Todd walks up to bat.

> **JANEY**
> *He's my brother.*

She lunges as if she plans to run onto the field again.

> **TODD**
> Eddie, help me out here.

Eddie grabs Janey by the waist.

> **JANEY**
> I can't let him rot in there, Todd. He's my one
> and only brother.

The wives of the opposing players are razzing the batters with "hey batta, batta ... miss, batta, batta."

TODD
There's no way on God's green earth we're
gonna pay that bail, Janey. No way.

Todd prepares to swing. Janey clings to the fence, razzing him:

JANEY
Hey, batta, batta, miss, batta, batta.

INT. JAIL CELL -- RAY AND SHERIFF -- SAME TIME
Ray is on his knees by his bunk, praying.

RAY
(muttering)
Lord Jesus, I know I ain't no count at all, Lord I
have never been a righteous man, I know I have
unholy thoughts and evil ways ...

ANGLE ON SHERIFF CLANCY
At the end of the cellblock hallway, listening.

ANGLE ON OTHER PRISONERS LISTENING

BACK TO RAY PRAYNING

RAY
... but Lord, I am your child, your child, that's
right. And that old Devil has his ways and his
powers, and life is hard, but oh Lord you are
more powerful, and you are perfect. *Perfect everything.*

CUT TO SHERIFF CLANCY
He shakes his head, walks away.

INT. SHERIFF'S OFFICE -- SHERIFF CLANCY
He returns to his office from the adjacent cellblock, and Lucy and
Cooper are waiting for him.

LUCY
How's he doin'?

SHERIFF
Oh, he's fine.

LUCY
Can I see him?

SHERIFF

Visiting hours are posted on the board there,
Lucy.

She turns to the bulletin board, reads.

LUCY

No exceptions?

SHERIFF

Sorry.

The Sheriff glances at Cooper.

COOPER

How much is bail?

SHERIFF

Five hundred.

COOPER

We don't have that much between us.

SHERIFF

Wouldn't matter now, judge won't be by until
morning to arraign him.

LUCY

Does that mean he's gotta spend the night here?

SHERIFF

That's right.

The Sheriff rises from his desk, walks up to Cooper.

SHERIFF

You know what, I'd like some hot coffee, what
about you folks?

He takes out some cash, hands a few bills to Cooper.

SHERIFF

I think the McDonalds out on 29 is still open.

COOPER

You don't have coffee here?

SHERIFF

I prefer Mickey D's.

COOPER

Okay, sure.

Cooper turns to leave and Lucy is about to follow, when;

SHERIFF

Wait, Lucy. Why don't you stay here. I've got something I'd like to ask you about, if you don't mind.

LUCY

Oh, okay. Get me a coffee, too, Coop, and one of them apple pies.

SHERIFF

Make that two apple pies.

COOPER
(weakly, feeling grossly manipulated)

No problem.

The Sheriff returns to his chair.

SHERIFF

Pull up a chair, Lucy.

Lucy drags a metal folding chair closer to the desk, sits down.

LUCY

What is it you wanted to ask me?

SHERIFF

It has to do with that fella Lester. He got beat up, remember? At The Inferno.

LUCY

I remember.

SHERIFF
You say you never saw him before, is that right?
Before that night he got beat up?

LUCY
No, I saw him at the hardware. He bought a
bucket.

SHERIFF
Hmmm. A bucket? Well. I went to see him,
when he was in the hospital. I sure did.

INT. HOSPITAL -- FLASHBACKS WITH SHERIFF AND LESTER
The Sheriff is in Lester's hospital room, but Lester is unconscious or
asleep and the Sheriff is snooping around, checking his wallet, etc.

SHERIFF (O.C.)
Nobody was ever charged in that assault, but
they should've been. Stump and them other
boys. Because Lester was in a bad way.

The Sheriff takes Lester's license, slips it into his shirt pocket.

CUT TO SHERIFF'S OFFICE -- FLASHBACK CONTINUES
The Sheriff walks to the computer, takes out Lester's license, and does a
search.

SHERIFF (O.C.)
I did a lookup on Lester's driver's license. His
name's Lester Hollis.

BACK TO PRESENT SCENE WITH SHERIFF AND LUCY

SHERIFF
Same last name as that boy you stabbed. The
one who raped you.

LUCY
Is that so.

CUT TO HOSPITAL -- SHERIFF AND LESTER -- ANOTHER DAY
Lester is awake now, head bandaged.

SHERIFF (O.C.)
I went back to talk to him, yessir, we had ourselves a nice long chat.

BACK TO CLOSE-UP OF LUCY IN PRESENT SCENE
Her gaze tightens as her mind absorbs the implications of his words ...

CUT BACK TO HOSPITAL FLASHBACK -- SHERIFF AND
LESTER TALKING

SHERIFF (O.C.)
He told me the whole story of what happened
that day.

BACK TO LUCY AND SHERIFF IN PRESENT SCENE

LUCY
How'd he know anything about it?

SHERIFF
Oh, he was there.

LUCY
He watched me gettin' raped? That's sick.

SHERIFF
I don't know about that, but what happened
after. The burning of the boy's body.

EXT. TRAILER -- LESTER IN THE WOODS
He is watching the trailer from a distance.

SHERIFF (O.C.)
He was there, Lucy, at the edge of the woods.
He saw everything.

CUT TO THE DOOR OF THE HOUSE (OR TRAILER)
Lucy and Ray carry Larry, with a large knife sticking out of his chest, out
the front door of the trailer and around the back of the trailer.

RAY
You got him? Don't drop him.

LUCY
Daddy, we're spilling blood everywhere.

RAY

I guess we shoulda wrapped him in a sheet or something. Hell, girl, you must've stuck that knife right through his heart.

LUCY

I think I might have, daddy.

INSERT FLASHBACK OF LUCY STABBING HIM (INT. TRAILER BEDROOM -- LUCY AND LARRY)

Like a moment frozen in time -- Lucy has already stuck the knife into Larry. He is lying on the bed and his eyes are open and he is gripping her by the hair with one hand, her face contorted, but she clings to the knife stuck in the center of his chest until he loosens his grip. She shakes her head, throwing her hair back so she can see and looks down at the blood puddling on his chest.

BACK TO FLASHBACK OF THE BODY DISPOSAL

They have stuffed Larry's body inside the barrel used for burning trash out behind the trailer. He is stuck down into it real good with only his head protruding.

CUT TO LESTER WATCHING FROM THE WOODS

Strangely dumbfounded and paralyzed like he's watching a bad movie.

BACK TO LUCY AND RAY WITH LARRY'S BODY

Ray douses the body with gasoline, then:

LUCY

Daddy, what about the knife?

RAY

What do ya mean?

LUCY

It's the murder weapon, shouldn't we throw it away or something?

RAY

You are one smart girl, pun'kin.

LUCY

Daddy, I hate it when you call me pun'kin.

RAY
Okay sweetness. I 'spose we'll have to take that
knife out of him.

CUT TO LESTER WATCHING

BACK TO THE SCENE
Ray steps toward the barrel.

LUCY
You gonna do it, daddy?

RAY
I 'spose I am.

He reaches for the knife.

BACK TO THE SHERIFF'S OFFICE IN PRESENT TIME

SHERIFF
You want to tell me how it went down?

CLOSE-UP OF LUCY
Unflinching, stoic.

BACK TO SHERIFF

SHERIFF
Do ya, Lucy? I think its time you told me the
truth.

CUT BACK TO THE HOSPITAL WITH SHERIFF AND LESTER

SHERIFF
Because, you see, I know the truth. From Lester.

CLOSE-UP OF LESTER TELLING THE STORY

CUT TO CLOSE-UP OF LESTER WATCHING FROM WOODS

CLOSE-UP OF RAY REACHING FOR THE KNIFE

WIDER ANGLE ON RAY, LUCY AND LARRY
Ray grips the knife, yanks it out ...

CLOSE-UP OF LARRY'S EYES POPPING OPEN
He gasps. Ray gasps.

CUT TO RAY AND LUCY

LUCY
(screaming)
Oh god, he's alive! Daddy, he's alive!

CUT TO CLOSE-UP OF LESTER IN THE WOODS
As he gasps.

BACK TO RAY AND LUCY

RAY
Did you hear something?

LUCY
No. Maybe it was a squirrel.

Ray listens for a moment, seems content that it was nothing.

BACK TO LESTER
As he quietly backs further into shadow.

CUT TO RAY AND LUCY AND LARRY
Ray lights a match.
LUCY
Daddy?

CLOSE-UP OF LARRY
Larry's eyes are wide open but he can't speak, it's like he's petrified, yet in his eyes he is questioning, pleading ...

BACK TO RAY AND LUCY

RAY
I know, son. I know.

Ray tosses the match onto Larry and he goes up in flames, SCREAM-ING IN AGONY, his voice carrying over to the next shot.

BACK TO PRESENT SCENE IN SHERIFF'S OFFICE

SHERIFF
(first, a beat, as Larry's scream fades)
That's what happened, am I right, Lucy?

ANGLE ON COOPER ENTERING
With coffee and pies.

NEW ANGLE ON THE THREE

> **LUCY**
> Oh, thank God, Coop. I was dying for a coffee.

Cooper hands the Sheriff a coffee.

> **COOPER**
> Sheriff.

Cooper pulls up a chair beside Lucy's.

> **COOPER**
> This is nice, isn't it. Hope the coffee's still hot.

> **SHERIFF**
> Mine is.

> **LUCY**
> Mine is, too.

EXT. COOPER'S TRAILER -- LUCY -- DAY
Lucy drives up in Harold's car. (She has just delivered food to Samson's family.) She has been crying. She gets out of the car. BALDO and some of the other Mexican construction workers are hanging out.

> **BALDO**
> Hey Lucy, how's it going?

> **LUCY**
> Hey Baldo.

She knocks on Cooper's trailer door.

> **LUCY**
> Coop? Coop?

> **BALDO**
> He's not here.

Lucy tries the door on the trailer and goes inside.

INT. COOPER'S TRAILER -- LUCY

She goes to the fridge and gets a beer. She sits down on the sofa adjacent to the front door. BALDO appears -- he's ten feet from the door, just checking on her. She waves.

> **BALDO**
>
> You okay, Lucy?

> **LUCY**
>
> No. My friend Samson ... his wife is about to die.

> **BALDO**
>
> I'm so sorry.

> **LUCY**
>
> Yeah.

She takes a sip of beer, sets the bottle down, gets up and goes to the bathroom.

INT. BATHROOM -- LUCY

She looks at herself in the mirror, then she breaks down, as if she can cry safely in the privacy of the bathroom. She leans her head against the mirror of the medicine cabinet. When she pulls her head back, the medicine cabinet swings open. She glances at what's inside -- some prescription medicines. She picks one up and looks at it. The name on it isn't Cooper Daniels. It's David Little. Lucy backs up, staring at the bottle, then she sets it back inside the medicine chest and closes the mirror.

INT. COOPER'S BEDROOM -- LUCY

She enters, looks around. She opens the small closet, goes through his modest wardrobe, then she reaches onto the top shelf and finds a handgun in a Pelican case. She sits on the bed and opens the case. It contains a nickel-plated Glock. Tucked into the edge of the case there's an ID card. She pulls it out and looks at it. It says FEDERAL AGENT -- I.N.S. Her eyes grow wide.

> **LUCY**
>
> Baldo!

EXT. COOPER'S TRAILER -- NEAR DUSK

Cooper pulls up on his motorcyle. None of the Mexican workers are anywhere around. Lucy is sitting on the trailer's front stoop.

>   **COOPER**
>   Lucy, what's wrong? Where is everybody?

Lucy throws his I.N.S. ID at his feet.

>   **COOPER**
>   I wanted to tell you. I swear I did.

>   **LUCY**
>   Becky's going to die, pro'bly tonight. I think I'll
>   go see how Samson's doing.

Lucy walks past him to the car.

EXT. TODD & JANEY'S HOUSE -- COOPER & TODD -- LATER
Cooper walks to the front door and knocks. Todd answers the door.

>   **COOPER**
>   Todd Benson, you're under arrest for employing
>   illegal aliens.

>   **TODD**
>   You son of a bitch.

>   **COOPER**
>   Sorry buddy. Just doing my job.

INT. JAIL CELL -- RAY, TODD, SHERIFF & COOPER -- LATER
Cooper and the Sheriff usher Todd into the cell where Ray resides. After
locking the door, Cooper and the Sheriff walk down the cellblock.

>   **RAY**
>   Todd, what'd you do?

>   **TODD**
>   They busted me for hiring illegal aliens.

>   **RAY**
>   Is that a crime?

>   **COOPER**
>   **(from the end of the hallway)**
>   You better believe it's a crime.

>   **TODD**
>   Shut up! You know those men need jobs.
>   They're your friends for Christsake!

79

Cooper pauses at the door to the cellblock, listens to Todd.

TODD
Hell, those guys just want a better life. You can't
blame a man for wanting that!

Cooper exits through the door, then the Sheriff returns, pausing in the
doorway.

SHERIFF
You boys need anything? (beat) I didn't think so.

He closes the door.

BACK TO TODD AND RAY

TODD
Well this is something, huh, Ray. We're some bad
pair of desperadoes. You ran over a cat, and I
hired a few Mexicans. Damn.

INT. LUCY'S APARTMENT -- LUCY, CARLA & COOPER -- DAY
Carla and Lucy are making sandwiches when Cooper knocks.

LUCY
It's open.

CARLA
You've got some nerve.

COOPER
I want to talk to Lucy. Lucy?

A minute later, Lucy and Cooper are in the bedroom.

LUCY
Who the hell are you really?

INT. SHERIFF'S OFFICE -- LUCY AND SHERIFF -- LATER
Lucy walks in looking anxious, worried.

LUCY
Daddy still here?

SHERIFF

Yeah, he's in there keeping Todd company. I guess you heard.

LUCY

Oh yeah, I heard.

SHERIFF

That Cooper's something.

LUCY

He had me fooled. I got the bail for Daddy.

She drops a wad of cash on the Sheriff's desk.

SHERIFF

This is supposed to go to the Clerk.

LUCY
(**sarcastically**)

Well, where's the *Clerk?*

SHERIFF

She's not here right now.

LUCY

Well damn.

SHERIFF

Lucy, look, you know this is none of my doin'.

LUCY
(**thinking**)

It's not?

SHERIFF

This stuff with Todd and the Mexicans? Hell no. I could care less. (beat) Look, I'll go ahead and let Ray out.

He gets the cell keys and walks toward the cellblock. Lucy follows him.

LUCY
What about the Clerk?

SHERIFF
Don't worry about that.

INSIDE THE CELLBLOCK -- SHERIFF AND LUCY
As he opens the door and they enter the cellblock.

SHERIFF
You're not supposed to come back here.

LUCY
I want to see Uncle Todd.

SHERIFF
Oh, what the hell, come on.

ANOTHER ANGLE -- SHERIFF, LUCY, TODD AND RAY
Both men stand as the Sheriff and Lucy approach.

SHERIFF
You're out of here, Ray.

TODD
What about me?

The Sheriff unlocks the cell door and lets Ray out.

LUCY
I didn't have enough money for you, too, Uncle
Todd. Sorry. Have you talked to Janey?

Todd rests his forehead against the bars.

TODD
Yeah, I talked to her. We're short of capital
thanks to her giving two thousand dollars to the
Resurrection Temple.

RAY
Janey will get her reward.

TODD

It was my money, too, so I should get a reward. (beat) (to Lucy) Janey will raise my bail eventually. She'll sell my truck or my guns or something else I cherish.

LUCY

Well ... bye.

Lucy leans over and kisses his cheek.

LUCY

I love you.

She turns to follow the Sheriff and Ray, then turns back.

TODD

Cooper's an asshole and I hate him.

LUCY

Well, it was his job, Uncle Todd.

Lucy runs down the cellblock and throws her arm around Ray's neck. Sheriff Clancy pauses, looks over his shoulder at Todd.

SHERIFF

You good?

TODD

Oh yeah. *Great.*

EXT. ROAD -- LUCY AND RAY ON THE SCOOTER -- LATER
Lucy's red hair trails behind them like a banner.

INT. INFERNO -- LUCY AND RAY -- LATER
Hardly anybody else is in the joint except Ben, the bartender. Ray and Lucy sit at a table.

RAY

Set us up, Ben, a bottle of Old Number Seven with its stamp on.

LUCY

And a beer.

Ben brings a bottle of Jack Daniels, two glasses and a glass of ice. They pour and drink. Lucy notices how much Ray seems to need the alcohol.

LUCY

Lester, the hillbilly, he's Larry's brother.

Ray wears a quizzical look.

LUCY

You know, the one we killed. Larry?

RAY

Golly, I 'bout forgot his name. Maybe it was a memory I needed to put out of my head.

INSERT -- CU OF LARRY IN BARREL (FLASHBACK)
THEN, TILT UP FROM MATCH TO RAY'S FACE

BACK TO SCENE IN INFERNO WITH LUCY AND RAY

LUCY

Daddy, you're all the time talkin' about life after death, and going to heaven, but *my life*, after *Larry's death*, ain't been for shit.

RAY

We'll get through, darlin', with some help from upstairs. Come on, I want to show you something.

INT. CHURCH -- RAY AND LUCY -- LATER
He turns on the lights. The "sanctuary" is in order -- mostly old chairs and a couple of tattered sofas, and there's a pulpit made out of unfinished two by fours.

LUCY

You got it all fixed up didn't you.

RAY

God's been real good. He's been good to you and me.

LUCY

I guess he's been good to us. In his own way.

84

RAY
I think so. I do. This is our new start.

Ray picks up a hand painted "Services Tonite 7:00" sign and walks out the front door. Lucy follows him.

EXT. CHURCH -- RAY AND LUCY
Ray puts the sign near the road while Lucy lights a cigarette.

EXT. TODD & JANEY'S HOUSE -- THAT NIGHT
Through a window, Todd can be seen reading the newspaper, the TV flickering across the room.

TODD (V.O.)
The end to Lucy and Ray's story isn't pretty.

INT. LUCY'S APARTMENT -- LUCY
She sits in a big upholstered chair, sets a beer on the table beside it, and picks up her white Bible, opens it and reads.

TODD (V.O.)
But I guess we all have to face who we are, and
I mean deep inside where it gets dark. Same for
Lucy.

INT. SAMSON'S HOUSE -- SAMSON & FRIENDS
Everyone has gathered at the small shack of a house after Becky's funeral. SAMSON and HAROLD and the PASTOR are there, along with LUCY and SUZY.

TODD (V.O.)
By God's grace, we will survive whatever it is we
need to, each with his cross to bear.

SUZIE
(to Samson)
Have you found a job yet?

SAMSON
I did get a job. At the Walmart over in Liberty.

LUCY
That's awesome!

She gives him a big hug.

INT. CHURCH -- RAY & OTHERS

Ray is preaching up a storm. There are a few people in attendance: Janey is there. Also, an old black man and three black women, and a family of tourists with a toddler.

TODD (O.C.)
Personally, I'm not a religious man. I'll leave the preaching to Ray. He has the energy for it.

NEW ANGLE ON RAY

He reaches for a shotglass of whiskey on the pulpit (as Primitive Baptists have been known to do), gulps it, and keeps preaching.

INT. RAY'S APARTMENT INSIDE THE CHURCH -- SAME TIME

Beams of light hit Ray where he sleeps on a cot in a back room.

CAMERA JIBS IN CLOSER UNTIL HE OPENS HIS EYES

Eyes ablaze with wonder: he has had a most momentous dream.

EXT. CHURCH -- RAY -- A FEW MINUTES LATER

Ray stands in his cowboy boots, boxer shorts and a wife beater out in front of the former tire center. He holds his Bible and is transfixed, staring at the vacant lot next door.

SUZIE'S P.O.V. DRIVING

Suzie is about to drive by when she sees Ray. She pulls over and gets out.

SUZIE
Ray, what's going on? Ray?

She looks at the sign on the front of the church that Lester painted.

SUZIE Cont'd
I think there's a spelling problem, Ray.

RAY
(without looking at her)
I know, Suzie, but its growing on me.

SUZIE
Ray, why don't you put the Bible away. You know you don't really believe any of that.

RAY

Yes I do. I surely do. And even if I didn't it
would still be true.

SUZIE

Ray, have you finally lost it?

RAY

Good God in heaven, Suzie, I had a dream
last night. A revelation. I am going to build an
eighteen hole Jesus Putt-Putt right there. Right
there, and every hole will teach a vital verse from
the testaments old and new. The whole story of
redemption spread out perfect on bright green
plastic turf. We'll put up signs on 29 and pull
thousands of tourists right off the highway.

She pats him on the shoulder as if he was a child.

SUZIE

You never fail to surprise me, Ray.

RAY

Suzie, God's surprised me this time.

EXT. SHERIFF'S OFFICE -- SHERIFF AND JANEY -- SAME TIME
As the Sheriff walks to the door, Janey runs up to him.

JANEY

Carl, I want my husband.

SHERIFF

Well let's go get him.

EXT. SUZIE'S CAFE -- SUZIE AND HAROLD -- THAT MORNING
Suzie goes to the front door and sees that it is open.

INT. SUZIE'S CAFE -- SUZIE
Suzie enters, looks around, then she HEARS HAROLD coming in the
back door.

SUZIE

Harold?

HAROLD
It's me.

SUZIE
Have you seen Lucy?

HAROLD
No I haven't.

He walks into the dining room.

HAROLD
Was she supposed to open up?

SUZIE
Yes. The front door was wide open.

Harold sees a Polaroid camera on the counter, half hidden behind the donut display. A photo is hanging out of it. He picks up the photo.

SUZIE
What's that?

HAROLD
It's a picture ...

He hands it to Suzie.

SUZIE'S P.O.V. OF THE POLAROID PHOTO
It's a picture of Lucy with duct tape over her mouth, being held by Lester as he extends his arm to take the picture. The door suddenly opens, making Suzie gasp and jump. CUT TO:

SAMSON ENTERING THE FRONT DOOR
Carrying a box of big red tomatoes.

SUZIE
Oh my god.

BACK TO SUZIE
She looks up from the photo.

SUZIE
Samson ... what do you want?

NEW ANGLE ON SCENE
Harold takes the picture from Suzie, studies it, pacing. Samson sets the
tomatoes on the counter.

SAMSON
I brought over some tomatoes to say thank you.
(beat) Something wrong?
(to Harold)
What's going on, Captain?

Harold slides the photo down the counter where it sticks under the edge
of the cardboard box of tomatoes. Samson squints at it, then looks up at
Suzie, his face contorted by an expression of deep concern.

EXT. CHURCH -- SUZIE AND SAMSON -- LATER
Suzie drives into the parking lot, she and Samson get out of the car
quickly. The front door is open ...

INT. CHURCH SANCTUARY -- RAY, SUZIE & SAMSON
Ray is painting the pulpit with lime green paint.

SUZIE
Ray, Lucy's been kidnapped.

Ray turns from his work.
RAY
What?

He brushes his hair back, leaving a smear of paint on his forehead.

INT. SHERIFF'S OFFICE -- COOPER & SHERIFF -- SAME TIME
Cooper enters and walks to the Sheriff's desk, where Sheriff Clancy is
reading a magazine.

COOPER
I'm going to Raleigh for a few days. Just wanted
you to know.

SHERIFF
Oh really, why is that?

COOPER
Hey, I understand how you feel. This is your
domain.

SHERIFF
You're damn straight.

COOPER

And you probably don't worry too much about
illegals?

SHERIFF

No, them fellas are not a high priority when I
have meth labs and pot growers to worry about.

COOPER

How's your buddy doing?

SHERIFF

Todd? He'll survive this little case of hickups.

CUT TO TODD AND JANEY
They have just walked in from the Clerk's office. Janey clings to Todd's
arm as if all has been forgiven.

TODD

Well look who's here.
(**waving the bail receipt**)
You're costing me a lot of money, boy.

The Sheriff hands Todd a brown envelope containing his wallet, cell
phone, loose change, etc.

COOPER

Just applying the law, that's all I'm doing. You
want this country to be overrun by illegal aliens?

Cooper looks at Todd, then at the Sheriff.

COOPER

Somebody's got to do something.

NEW ANGLE ON SCENE
RAY, SUZIE and SAMSON enter.

RAY

Carl, Lester's taken Lucy.

SHERIFF

Taken her where?

Suzie hands the photo to the Sheriff. Todd, Janey and Cooper look over
his shoulder.

JANEY
Oh god.

SHERIFF
What'd he do that for?

SUZIE
Turn it over.

CLOSE-UP OF THE BACK SIDE OF THE POLAROID
Lester has scrawled: "Gimee precher."

JANEY
He means *preacher.*

SHERIFF
That's you, Ray.

TODD
What are we going to do, Carl?

SHERIFF
We'll go get her. Question is, where'd that lunatic
take her?

SAMSON
You got a map?

INSERT OF MAP BEING UNFURLED ON THE SHERIFF'S DESK

THE SHERIFF'S OFFICE -- A FEW MOMENTS LATER
Everyone is gathered around the map.

SAMSON
That boy's homeplace is up in the hills a quarter
mile or so from my place.

COOPER
How do you know he's taken her there?

SAMSON
I don't for absolute.

SHERIFF
Boys, I'm not going on a wild goose chase ...

Todd's CELL PHONE RINGS. He reaches inside the envelope, slips the phone out, answers it.

CLOSE-UP OF LUCY ON HER CELL PHONE
She looks a little freaked out.

LUCY

Uncle Todd?

BACK TO GROUP IN SHERIFF'S OFFICE
Todd's eyes grow wide. He clicks the phone to speaker so everyone can hear ...

TODD

Lucy? You okay, honey?

LUCY

He's got me at an old farm.

Ray gives Samson a congratulatory slap on the back.

TODD

What does he want, Lucy?

BACK TO LUCY
Glancing at Lester, then:

LUCY

He wants daddy.

TODD

Okay, Red.

NEW ANGLE ON LUCY AND LESTER
Lester grabs her phone and flings it against the wall. The phone smashes to pieces but continues to work.

TODD AND OTHERS (O.S.)

Lucy? Lucy? Are you there? Lucy? We're coming
for you, honey.

Lester walks over and crushes the remains of the phone under the weight of a brogan.

BACK TO THE SCENE IN SHERIFF'S OFFICE -- JUMP TO:
Sheriff handing out rifles from the rifle case. He hands one to Cooper, and one to Ray.

SAMSON
Give me one, captain.

SHERIFF
You sure?

Samson nods resolutely.

SHERIFF
Toddy?

TODD
(to Janey)
Did you drive the truck?

JANEY
Yes.

EXT. PARKING LOT AT SHERIFF'S OFFICE -- TODD'S TRUCK
He grabs his deer rifle off the gun rack and starts loading rounds.

NEW ANGLE -- THE MEN MAKING UP THE "POSSE"
The posse: the Sheriff, Ray, Cooper, Samson and Todd.

JANEY
(kissing Todd)
Be careful.

SUZIE
You boys don't do anything foolish.

They climb into the Sheriff's cruiser and Todd's truck and drive away.

EXT. HIGHWAY -- THREE VEHICLES -- LATER
Raleigh joins them going down the highway and all three vehicles pull off onto a dirt road.

ANOTHER ANGLE ON THE CARS ON A DIRT ROAD
As they speed along.

EXT. HOLLIS FARM -- SAME TIME
An old house, and an old barn -- a quiet, beatific, badly overgrown farm.

LESTER'S FATHER ON THE PORCH
The old man sits on the porch, plucking his banjo.

INT. HOLLIS HOUSE -- LESTER AND LUCY -- AFTERNOON
They are in the front room and the banjo can still be heard outside on the porch. Through the open window, the old man's arm is visible where he sits. Lester opens a cooler, gets a soda, offers Lucy a sandwich.

> **LUCY**
> What kind is it?

> **LESTER**
> Bologna n' mustard.

> **LUCY**
> Yum. You make it?

> **LESTER**
> Yup.

Lester puts a soda and bologna sandwich on the window ledge.

> **LESTER**
> Pop?

The old man reaches back and gets his soda and sandwich.

> **LUCY**
> **(chewing)**
> Not bad.

Lester squints, then smiles at her compliment. SFX: CARS FAST APPROACHING.

EXT. HOLLIS HOUSE -- ANGLES ON THE POSSE PULLING UP
The Sheriff pulls up, along with Todd, the men get out cautiously. The Sheriff carries a bull horn and his own deer rifle. They approach the old farmhouse stealthily.

> **SHERIFF**
> Easy now boys. Let's split up. Left and right.

They split up -- Ray, Samson and Cooper go right. Todd, Raleigh and the Sheriff stay to the left, using cover as they approach the farmhouse.

COOPER
Who's that old man?

SAMSON
He's the old moonshiner who lives here.

Sheriff Clancy raises the bullhorn to his mouth.

SHERIFF
Lester, you in there?

LESTER'S FATHER
Go away.

SHERIFF
Old man, we're not going anywhere without Lucy. Is Lester in there?

LESTER
I got the girl!

SHERIFF
Okay. We understand. I prefer we do some talkin' first, to see if we can work this out without nobody gettin' hurt. Lester?

INT. HOLLIS HOUSE -- LESTER AND LUCY

LESTER
(to Lucy)
There's a bunch of 'em.

LUCY
Good. (calling) Come and get me, boys!

LESTER
Girl, shut your trap!

ANGLE ON RALEIGH
Crouching low, he walks behind the Sheriff, about to move to a forward position.

RALEIGH
I'm movin' up closer.

The Sheriff's expression reveals that he does not approve of Raleigh's decision.

NEW ANGLE ON RALEIGH
As he creeps closer.

INT. HOLLIS HOUSE -- TIGHT SHOT OF LESTER
Lester raises his rifle and fires at Raleigh.

BACK TO RALEIGH
He hits the ground like a sack of rocks.

ANGLE ON LUCY

LUCY
Oh my God, you shot him.

In the background Lester's father walk by, leaving the front door open.

ANGLE ON TODD AND THE SHERIFF

TODD
Holy shit.

SHERIFF
That boy can shoot.

BACK TO LESTER
He slams the door shut.

LESTER
I got one of yours boys!
(to himself)
Got him clean.

ANGLE ON COOPER

COOPER
Lucy, we're here for you, baby.

BACK TO LESTER
He fires at Cooper and hits him in the side of the head.

ANGLE ON LUCY
Springing toward Lester like a wild cat.

LUCY
(screaming)
You asshole, I'm going to kill you!

She jumps on Lester and he punches her, throwing her backward, her lip busted.

CUT TO COOPER
Moaning, holding his head, blood streaming between his fingers.

CUT TO RALEIGH
Groaning pain.

CLOSE-UP OF LESTER
He draws a bead on Cooper, a kill shot to the head, then he decides not to take it. (Remembering how Cooper helped him that night.)

ANGLE ON SAMSON AND RAY

SAMSON
That deputy's hurt bad.

NEW ANGLE ON SAMSON -- LESTER'S FATHER P.O.V.
From an upstairs window. Samson runs out to get Raleigh, starts pulling him to safety ...

ANGLE ON THE OLD MAN LOOKING OUT THE WINDOW

CUT TO LESTER
He takes aim and fires at Samson.

CUT BACK TO SAMSON
Samson is hit and falls backward. Ray rushes forward and grabs Samson, pulls him backward to cover, and checks out his wound, which is rather grievous.

ANGLE ON LUCY
Upon seeing that Samson got shot, too.

LUCY
(weakly)
You hit him, didn't you.

Lester nods.

LUCY Cont'd
I hate your guts.

LESTER
Ever'body hates me.

LUCY
Why do you think that is?

LESTER
I always wondered.

BACK TO RAY, SAMSON AND COOPER
Cooper's body makes a strange dying noise. Ray is trying to stop Samson's bleeding, getting blood all over his hands.

RAY
(to Samson)
Put your hand there, press down on it.
(to Lester)
Okay boy, here I am. It's me you want, ain't that right?

He walks a few steps then sinks to his knees and moves forward "walking" on his knees. There's a red stain on his shirt where the old shiv wound has opened.

RAY
I lay down my life. Now let Lucy go.

BACK TO LESTER AND LUCY

LESTER
Go on.

LUCY
Really?

LESTER
Git on outta here, Lucy.

EXT. HOLLIS HOUSE -- NEW ANGLE ON LUCY
She walks out, then runs.

RAY
(as she runs by)
Run girl.

NEW ANGLE -- SAMSON, COOPER AND LUCY
As she gets to them.

BACK TO RAY
Walking on his knees closer and closer to Lester.

ANGLE ON LESTER

LESTER
Wait.

RAY
What do you want now?

LESTER
Why'd you do it?

RAY
Your brother sinned against my daughter. He
sinned, Lester.

Ray moves closer.

LESTER
Me n' papa, we knowed he was evil.

RAY
Don'tcha see, son, the grave is open like a door
... it's on us to decide on heaven or hell. God's
not the judge. No sir, we condemn ourselves.

LESTER
But it was you killed him, and you ain't God.

RAY
No, son, I am anything but.

Ray's so close, Lester is suffering parallax, seeing double images. He
struggles to aim, fires, hits Ray in the shoulder.

NEW ANGLE ON RAY
He leans backward, then topples slowly to the side, clutching his shoulder.

ANGLE ON SHERIFF AND TODD
They open fire on Lester. There is no return fire. A moment passes.

SHERIFF
(using the bullhorn)
Lester? Lester?

The Sheriff looks at Todd. They stand and approach tentatively. The Sheriff crouches beside Ray, who looks up at him with tender eyes.

RAY
I forgive him, Carl.

SHERIFF
That's right big of you, Ray.

INT. HOLLIS HOUSE -- SHERIFF AND TODD
The two men walk through the farmhouse. Lester is gone.

NEW ANGLE ON TODD IN THE FARMHOUSE KITCHEN
Todd opens the back door, Sheriff Clancy joins him there.

THEIR P.O.V. OF LESTER
Running through a meadow out back of the house.

TODD (O.C.)
There he goes.

CUT TO TODD -- THEN THE SHERIFF
Todd steps into the yard and takes aim with his deer rifle. The Sheriff steps up beside him, takes aim.

BACK TO LESTER
He sees them and stops, raises his rifle ...

CUT TO TODD AND THE SHERIFF
They fire almost simultaneously.

BACK TO LESTER
He crumples to the ground.

ANGLE ON LESTER'S FATHER
watching from a second story window.

ANOTHER ANGLE ON TODD AND SHERIFF CLANCY
They walk casually through the meadow, and everything is quiet except for the sound of their feet swishing through the tall grass.

DISTANT ANGLE ON TODD AND SHERIFF CLANCY
They stop, standing over Lester.

CLOSE-UP OF LESTER
Shot through in two places, hurting, breathing heavy.

NEW ANGLE ON TODD AND SHERIFF CLANCY
as they look at each other.

ANGLE ON LUCY AND RAY
as they hear a gunshot in the distance.

CUT TO LESTER'S FATHER IN THE WINDOW
watching his son die.

FADE TO BLACK

FADE UP:

EXT. GRAVEYARD -- SHERIFF, TODD AND A GRAVE DIGGER
Sheriff Clancy and Todd walk past a guy sitting on a backhoe, smoking a
Chesterfield. They walk to the open grave of Lester Hollis.

> **TODD (V.O.)**
> Lester was buried in potter's field beside his
> brother's bones. Just me and Carl were there.

NEW ANGLE ON THE WOODS -- AND LESTER'S FATHER
watching from afar, hidden by the foilage.

EXT. HOUSE BUILDING SITE -- TODD & HIGH SCHOOL BOYS
Todd has a crew of inept teenagers working for him.

ANGLE ON A TEENAGE LABORER
As he hits his thumb with a hammer and screams in pain.

> **TODD**
> I paid a thousand dollar fine and went right back
> to building houses, only I had to hire high school
> kids.

NEW ANGLE -- ANOTHER TEENAGE LABORER
as he accidently nails his boot to a rafter.

101

EXT. SUZIE'S DINER -- LUCY, DINER GIRLS & HAROLD -- DAY
Lucy hugs and kisses Suzie, Val, Gloria and Harold goodbye.

> **TODD**
> Lucy eventually moved away with Cooper. She
> found something more than our tasteless chaw of
> a town could give her. I'm glad for she did.

INT. CHURCH -- RAY PREACHING
His small congregation seems lethargic and bored.

> **TODD**
> Ray kept on with his church 'til his congregation
> figured him out. Then he left town, too.

INT. TV STUDIO -- RAY -- ANOTHER DAY
He is gettting into makeup for his TV show.

> **TODD**
> We see him on the TV now and again where he'll
> live eternally, I guess, pointing out our sins
> as if we don't know them well enough already.

EXT. FOREST -- TODD AND SHERIFF CLANCY
They walk along wearing camouflage, guns on their shoulders.

> **TODD**
> We're expecting a Walmart soon. I guess we'll
> just grin stupidly and bear it. America, what a
> spectacle we've become.

EXT. WALMART GARDEN CENTER -- TODDY AND SAMSON
Samson helps Todd load some plants into his truck.

> **TODD**
> Sometimes it seems people have got beyond reach
> of each other. But not here, not in this little town.
> Here, we look out for each other.

EXT. TODD AND JANEY'S BACKYARD -- TODD AND JANEY
A warm, sunny afternoon. The barbecue smokes with hamburgers. Janey
brings out a tray of condiments and drinks. Todd sits at the picnic table.

TODD

Janey says she's not too old to have a baby. Who knows, maybe we'll try again. It would make her happy. It would give us something to live for, right? Everybody needs that.

THE END

Also by John Leslie Butchart:

The Music We're Born Remembering

Sons of Noah

Elyana

- novels -

Lake of Fire

The Hive

- motion pictures -

The Theory of Everything & Beyond

- nonfiction -

On the web:

www.lesbutchart.website
Author Page at Amazon

About the Author

John Leslie Butchart was born in Greensboro, NC, and attended the University of North Carolina at Chapel Hill where he studied creative writing, psychology and filmmaking.

He and his wife Susan have a movie production company, Highway 29 Motion Pictures.

John is also the founder of *Movies Among Friends*, a North Carolina motion picture group formed to develop independent films, and the founder of New River Releasing.

He has written more than twenty screenplays, and three novels: *The Music We're Born Remembering, Sons of Noah, and Elyana.*

His feature film productions include *Esposito, Elephant Sighs,* and *Lake of Fire,* a southern gothic tale, which he wrote and directed.

www.ingramcontent.com/pod-product-compliance
Lightning Source LLC
Chambersburg PA
CBHW070344130626
46556CB00007B/3023